Caleb had never kissed a woman before. . . .

He wanted to go on kissing Lucy, but he felt her pull away a bit. "Did I hurt you?" he muttered in a hoarse whisper.

Keeping her face turned away, she shook her head. Was she crying? Caleb touched Lucy's chin with his fingers and turned her to face him. Her face was wet with tears, and his throat tightened. "What is it, Lucy?"

"Now you kiss me," she said softly. "Now when I've failed so miserably. I don't want your pity, Caleb. I want your love and your respect. You expected certain things from a wife, and I don't think I can ever meet those expectations."

"I don't have any expectations."

Lucy shook her head and knuckled away her tears. "You and Pa are building an empire here. An empire takes an empress, someone who can stand at your side and fight whatever comes without fear. Today has shown me I can never be that woman. I was wrong to think I could."

"This doesn't sound like the Lucy I know. I need you, Lucy. I just didn't realize it before." He twined a long curl around his finger.

"I wish that were true," she muttered.

He tried to pull her close again, but she stood and evaded his grasp.

COLLEEN COBLE and her husband, David, raised two great kids, David Jr., and Kara, and they are now knee-deep in paint and wallpaper chips as they restore a Victorian home. Colleen became a Christian after a bad car accident in 1980, when all her grandmother's prayers finally took root. She is very active at her church, where she sings and helps her husband with a Sunday school class. She writes inspirational romance because she believes that the only happily ever after is with God at the center. She now works as a church secretary but would like to eventually pursue her writing full-time.

HEARTSONG PRESENTS

Don't miss out on any of our super romances. Write to us at the following address for information on our newest releases and club membership.

Heartsong Presents Readers' Service
PO Box 721
Uhrichsville, OH 44683

The Cattle Baron's Bride

Colleen Coble

Heartsong Presents

For Steve and Paula Parks, my wonderful pastor and his precious wife, who have been there all these years to encourage and exhort.

Also for Lucile Campese in Wichita Falls, Texas who supplied with boxes of information about her beloved city. Any errors about the area are mine, not hers.

A note from the author:
I love to hear from my readers! You may correspond with me by writing:

> **Colleen Coble**
> **Author Relations**
> **PO Box 719**
> **Uhrichsville, OH 44683**

ISBN 1-58660-382-5

THE CATTLE BARON'S BRIDE

All Scripture quotations, unless otherwise noted, are taken from the King James Version of the Bible.

All of the characters and events in this book are fictitious. Any resemblance to actual persons, living or dead, or to actual events is purely coincidental.

Cover design by Robyn Martins.

PRINTED IN THE U.S.A.

one

Lucy Marsh trudged up the splintered steps to the apartment of the boardinghouse. Every bone in her body ached, and she longed to throw herself across the bed and have a good cry. The paltry ten dollars in her reticule was all the money she would have coming in until she found another job. Mrs. Hanson had been apologetic about letting her go, and Lucy understood it was hard times and not her work that necessitated firing her, but that didn't keep food on the table.

She sighed. Eighteen seventy-seven had been a bad year so far, but it was bound to get better. She tried to trust in God to provide, but days like this made it hard. Sometimes it seemed no matter how hard she tried to be everything she should be, everything that God should love, she ended up failing.

She paused outside the door. She didn't want the children to see her worry. With a deep breath, she pinned a smile on her face and turned the doorknob. Before she could push the door open, Amos Cramer's gruff voice stopped her.

"One moment, Miss Marsh," he panted, hurrying toward her. He was a large, red-faced man with sparse gray hair and a handlebar mustache. He parked himself in front of her door and wheezed, struggling to catch his breath.

Her back against the door, Lucy pressed back as far as she could to escape the strong odor of stale perspiration

5

that drifted toward her. She had tried to be kind to Mr. Cramer until he mistook her kindness for a romantic interest. Now she just tried to stay out of his way.

He crowded closer. "I'm afraid I have some bad news for you," he said. His muddy gaze slid avidly over her face and hair.

Lucy pressed tighter against the wall, though it gained her no space between the odious man and herself. What now? She didn't think she could take anymore bad news.

"I've decided to sell out and go back to New York," he said. "I've had an offer I can't refuse for this place. The new owner plans to tear it down and build a new restaurant here." He hesitated and rubbed his lips with a dirty handkerchief. "I'm afraid I must ask you to leave within the next seven days."

Lucy gasped. "A week? How can I find something else in a week?" Dismay flooded her limbs.

Amos shrugged. "I'm sorry, my dear. You might try that boardinghouse over on Lincoln Avenue. They might have an opening." He pursed his lips and raked her figure with his gaze before turning and waddling away.

A great lump rose in Lucy's throat, but she fought the tears with determination. She couldn't cry, not now. She straightened her shoulders and pushed open the door. Her three-year-old sister Eileen launched herself against Lucy's legs.

"Lucy, you was late," she said, sticking out her lower lip. "Jed has company."

Lucy looked toward the single chair in the one-room apartment. A man with gray hair and penetrating charcoal eyes sat regarding her calmly before standing to his feet.

There was something forbidding in his face, and Lucy gave a tiny gasp. Her gaze sought and found her brother, Jed. Twelve years old, he'd been a handful all year. His hangdog expression did nothing to calm her fears.

"Jed?"

"Uh, Lucy, this is—"

"I'll introduce myself," the gentleman interrupted. He strode toward her and stared into her eyes. "Luther Stanton of Wichita Falls, Texas," he said. He shifted his gray Stetson in his hands, then pointed it at Jed. "Your young brother is in a heap of trouble, Miss. He lifted my wallet. I thought he'd gotten away with it, but I happened to find him in the mercantile down the street. That red hair is hard to miss."

Stealing! "Jed, no!" she wailed. "How could you?" It was too much. She couldn't take another problem. She burst into tears and sat on the edge of the bed abruptly. She buried her face in her hands and sobbed. Her shoulders heaved as she tried to get her emotions under control. Finally raising her head, she was surprised to find Luther leaning on the gold head of his walking cane with a speculative look on his face. She gulped and swiped at her wet cheeks.

"I was of a mind to call the sheriff, or whatever you call the law around here, but the youngster persuaded me to talk to you first. I hesitated to bring more trouble on you when your brother explained that you were caring for him and young Eileen. Commendable! But I can see it is of no use. Only the law will stop young Jed; you obviously have no control over him." He clapped his hat on his head and started toward the door.

"Wait," Lucy cried. "Surely we can talk about this for a few moments." Her mind raced. What could she do? How could she convince him not to prosecute? She'd promised her parents to take care of Jed; she had to keep her word. "I could work to pay back the money," she began. "I'm an excellent housekeeper. Are you in need of a maid or perhaps a cook?" What else could she do?

Mr. Stanton turned and looked at her. That odd speculation was back on his face. The silence seemed to stretch interminably before he finally spoke. "I have both a cook and a housekeeper who've been with me for years," he said. "Tell me, Miss Marsh, are you a Christian woman?"

Lucy stared at him in bewilderment. "Why, yes Sir, I am."

He smiled. "I thought as much. God has led me here for a purpose." He squared his shoulders. "There's only one thing I'm in need of."

Her heart leapt with hope. "What would that be, Mr. Stanton? I'll do anything to keep Jed out of jail." She glanced at her brother and was gratified to see him standing with his head hanging in shame. Perhaps this whole episode would wake him up.

"My son needs a wife, Miss Marsh. Have you read in the Bible how Abraham sent a servant out to find a wife for Isaac?"

"Of course," Lucy said, her heart sinking before beginning a rapid beat against her chest. Surely, he didn't think. . .

"That was my main purpose for this trip, though my son has no idea of my mission. But I've found no one suitable. I think you will do nicely."

The words fell into the silence of the room like an explosion of dynamite. Lucy's limbs went weak, and she could hardly stand. The room spun, and she sat slowly on the edge of the bed.

"I can see you don't fancy the idea," Mr. Stanton said. "That's fine. I understand completely, but you must realize that young Jed will now have to come with me. Get your gear together, Jed."

"No, wait!" Lucy put out a shaking hand to stop him. "Is—is your son a Christian? Can you give me until tomorrow to at least pray about it?"

Mr. Stanton smiled slowly. "That just confirms the Lord's leading me here. As soon as I soon as I clapped eyes on you, something reared up inside me. I knew you were the right one for my Caleb. Yes, my boy is a Christian, and I can see you would need time to confirm this is God's will. Very well, I will return at precisely nine o'clock tomorrow morning for your decision." He put a hand on her shoulder. "I have my son's signature to act as his agent in all business matters for this trip, so if you agree, I will arrange a proxy marriage. Right after the ceremony, we'll leave for Texas. A train leaves at one o'clock tomorrow afternoon, and I aim to be on it with or without you." He clapped his hat on his head and turned toward the door.

When the door closed behind him, Lucy clenched her hands in her lap and turned to her brother. Too angry to speak, she just looked at him.

Jed swallowed hard and took a step back. "It was just a dare, Lucy. I didn't mean to do anything wrong. I would have given it back to him."

"A dare? You have ruined our lives over a dare, Jed? One of us will pay, either you with an eternity in jail or me in bondage to some man I've never met. A jail of a different sort." She buried her head in her hands. "Lord, help me," she whispered. There was no way out. She couldn't fail her parents and her brother.

❧

She tossed and turned all night as she pleaded with God for a way out. At three in the morning, she finally slid out of bed and lit a lantern. She opened her Bible to Genesis 12.

> *Now the LORD has said unto Abram, Get thee out of thy country, and from thy kindred, and from thy father's house, unto a land that I will shew thee: And I will make of thee a great nation, and I will bless thee, and make thy name great; and thou shalt be a blessing.*

A blessing? She could be a blessing? Peace washed over her in a warm blanket. God was behind this; it had to be so. Marriage was an honorable thing. And this had come at a time when she saw no way to support the children and herself. Marriage was something God had ordained, and Mr. Stanton said his son was a Christian. She closed her Bible and crawled back into bed with Eileen. She would marry this Caleb and make him a good wife. Caleb meant faithful. That thought comforted her.

❧

After a frantic morning, they all found themselves aboard the train heading west. Mr. Stanton had arranged for comfortable accommodations, but the luxury car couldn't still the trepidation in Lucy's heart. What had she done? She stared down at the simple gold band on her left hand. She was a married woman, and she'd never even met the man. What if he was cruel or physically repulsive to her? What if he expected her to come right to the marriage bed? She suppressed a shudder.

But she had had no choice. When she looked into Mr. Stanton's level gray eyes, she had known he meant what he said. He would summon the authorities if she didn't agree to the marriage. Why was he so set on finding a wife for his son anyway? Was Caleb so repugnant he couldn't find a wife for himself? Lucy shuddered, then relaxed as a sense of peace calmed her frantic heart. God had given her direction. She would trust Him.

Eileen nestled against her arm, her breathing deep and easy. Jed was next to the window, staring morosely out at the bleak winter landscape. He hadn't had much to say all day. Lucy knew he felt terrible about what his actions had caused. She had been too angry to talk to him since he explained why he'd stolen Mr. Stanton's wallet. She knew she had to forgive him, but it was hard to do, especially before she met this Caleb and her own fate. Jed had been thoughtless and irresponsible. She sighed and said a silent prayer for the strength to forgive her brother. God had forgiven her many times; could she do less?

Jed's red hair fell across his forehead, and his freckles stood out on his pale skin. Lucy felt a wave of love well up for him. He'd had a rough year. He and Papa had been so close. The trauma of seeing their parents swept away by a flood had devastated him. Jed had clung to a tree and watched the flood sweep Papa right past him. He'd tried to grab Papa's arm, but the raging river had carried him out of Jed's reach. In one crushing blow, they'd been orphaned. The bodies of their parents hadn't been recovered for three days. Jed hadn't been the same since.

Jed looked up gratefully when she began to talk to him, and by the time they reached Pittsburgh, he had relaxed and was sleeping. Lucy wished she could sleep, but the thought of what awaited her in Texas kept her staring into the swirling snow outside the window. Mr. Stanton tried to talk to her several times, but he gave up when she answered in monosyllables.

აა

Caleb pushed his broad-rimmed Stetson back on his forehead and leaned back in his saddle. Whew, what a day he'd had. He'd lost ten head of cattle from the frigid cold in the past twenty-four hours. He couldn't remember ever enduring cold like this. And snow! The most they usually got was an inch or two that quickly melted away, not six inches like that covering the ground now. Then his favorite bay mare, Skyler, had broken a leg and had to be put down. He still winced from that. Skyler had been with him since he was fifteen. She was aging but still a good cattle horse. It would be hard to replace her. His mount, Maxi, was a good workhorse, but Caleb didn't have the rapport with him that he'd enjoyed with Skyler.

Pa should have been home two days ago. A dart of worry kept Caleb on edge. He hoped this sudden and unusual snowstorm hadn't trapped Pa somewhere. Turning Maxi's head, he plodded toward the house. Smoke curled from the chimney, and his mouth watered at the aroma of stew that blew in with the smoke. It had been a long time since breakfast. He rode into the barn and curried Maxi before heading to the house.

Not for the first time, he wondered if he should take a wife. Someone strong and knowledgeable about cattle. The only one he knew of in the area who fitted that description was Margaret Hannigan, Luke's daughter. She was almost as tall as Caleb was himself and could rope a calf nearly as well, too. She was no beauty, but he tried to tell himself that had nothing to do with his reluctance. Still, the thought of staring at that horsy face of Margaret's over breakfast every morning for the next forty years was enough to quell any man's appetite.

He sighed and put his speculation away. Bounding up the steps, he had his hand on the door when he heard the rattle and clank of a wagon coming across the snow-covered meadow. He turned and shaded his eyes with one hand while he studied the approaching convoy. Three wagons. It had to be Pa with provisions. His spirits lifted. Supper wouldn't be such a lonely affair with Pa home. Percy, their cook, didn't talk much, and there had been no one to share his thoughts with.

As the wagons neared, he recognized his father's gray head. Caleb lifted a hand in greeting and went to meet him. The welcoming grin faded when he saw the young woman clinging desperately to the wagon seat beside his father. Her youth and beauty seemed to bring sudden color to a dreary landscape.

He stared harder. What had Pa done? With a sinking heart, he remembered his father's ramblings about the place needing a woman's touch. Pa had gone and gotten himself hitched to a young filly! This woman was young enough to be Pa's daughter and Caleb's sister. How could he do this? Caleb gritted his teeth. The little hussy probably took one look at Pa and saw him for a rich sucker. Well, if she thought she was getting any money out of this ranch, she was sadly mistaken.

Silently, he waited for his father to step down from the wagon and explain. Maybe he hadn't married her yet. Maybe there would be a chance to talk him out of such a fool notion. Caleb's thoughts were interrupted when his father enveloped him in a bear hug. Caleb tried to return the embrace, but his rising anger kept his shoulders stiff.

"Caleb, Boy, you did good while I was gone. We passed the south pasture and saw the herd there. They look fat and sassy." He gripped his son's arms and stared into his face. "Help Lucy down while I get her luggage." He didn't wait for an answer, but then he never did. Caleb was used to his father's peremptory tone.

Caleb suppressed a sigh and offered his hand to the young woman. Lucy, his father called her. She was a cute little thing. Tiny, barely five feet if he had to hazard a guess, with huge blue eyes and fine blond hair. He could see how she might get to someone inexperienced in dealing with a little gold digger like her. But he would make sure his father saw through her wiles.

She took his arm and nearly fell when she tried to step down. He caught her in his arms and the contact sent a shock of awareness through him. He hastily set her on her feet and backed away. "Miss Lucy," he said, tipping his hat.

She stared at him with those enormous blue eyes. He'd never seen eyes so big and blue. A man could get lost in those eyes. She caught her full, pink lips between perfect white teeth. Was that fear in her eyes? She had cause to fear him, he thought grimly. He'd see her packed up and heading east if it was the last thing he did.

He heard an excited shout and turned to look at the last

wagon. A boy of about twelve came bounding through the snow, his cheeks red from the cold. His amazingly red hair stood up on end, and he carried a little girl who looked like a tiny version of Lucy.

"Did you see how big everything looks out here, Lucy?" He turned his brown eyes on Caleb. "How far's the nearest neighbors, Mister?"

Caleb softened a bit at the lad's exuberance. "Nearest would be Mitchells', about two miles away. They have some young 'uns close to your age." He frowned. Why had he bothered to tell the boy about neighbors? It wasn't like he was going to be here long enough to make any friends. Who was this kid anyway?

As if she had read his mind, Lucy introduced him. "Uh, Mr. Stanton, this is my brother Jed and my sister Eileen."

Caleb shook the boy's hand brusquely and turned to lead the way to the house. That boy might be her brother, but he'd bet the little girl was her own daughter. Percy and Luke, the foreman, had come to help with the provisions and the luggage, and he followed them into the house. Lucy had a bit of difficulty walking through the heavy drifts of snow. Caleb's lip curled in contempt. What had Pa been thinking? If he wanted a wife, why hadn't he picked one that would be a real helpmeet like the Bible said? This pale lily wouldn't last long out here.

He took her elbow and helped her along near the house where the drift went clear up on the porch. She shot him a grateful look from those blue eyes again, and his heart sped up. *Stupid, stupid*, he told himself. He was much too cautious to be caught in her little web of deceit. Frowning, he glared at his pa's back. Was Pa getting senile? It wasn't like him to be taken in like that. Caleb would get him alone and point out a few facts to him.

Lucy sighed and sank into the rocker near the fire. She held out her arms for Eileen and took off the little girl's coat, then spread it out in front of the fireplace. Setting Eileen on her feet, Lucy stood to take off her own cloak, bonnet, and mittens. When she pulled her small, white hands from the mittens, his heart sank when he saw the plain gold band on her left hand. She'd gotten Pa to marry her! Pa always was a sucker for a hard luck story. And there was a hard luck story lurking here somewhere. Why did she have her brother and sister with her? She probably gave Pa some story about being an orphan. If little Eileen wasn't her own daughter, he'd eat his hat.

Caleb's eyes met hers, and he saw the fear in them again. He narrowed his eyes and stared her down with a contemptuous curl to his lips. She paled and looked away. Good. She'd better be afraid of him. He was about to be her worst nightmare. No one made a fool of a Stanton.

His father came into the room, rubbing his hands. "I'm famished. We haven't eaten anything since breakfast. Let's eat while it's hot."

"Aren't you going to introduce me properly?" Caleb asked.

"There's time for all that after supper," his father answered. He avoided Caleb's gaze. "After we eat a bowl of the stew, we'll have some coffee here in the parlor by the fire, and I'll explain everything."

Supper was a stilted affair. Caleb saw the glances Jed kept tossing his way. Lucy grew more strained and silent. Her knuckles were white from gripping her fork, and she kept her eyes trained on her plate throughout the entire meal. His father tried to draw her into the discussion several times, but she wouldn't look at him and answered in the briefest of words.

Finally, his father pushed back his chair and gave a satisfied sigh. "I missed that good grub of yours, Percy. Now how about some of your famous coffee? They just don't know how to make the stuff out east. Bring it to the parlor when it's ready." He stood and led the way down the hall to the parlor.

Lucy pleated her dress nervously. "Could I put Eileen to bed? She's exhausted."

"Of course, dear girl." Luther turned to Caleb. "Show her to the little guest room, Son. The coffee should be ready by the time you get back."

Caleb had been watching for an opportunity to talk to her alone all evening. He led her up the stairs and down the hall, swinging open the door to the smallest guest room. Silently, Lucy slipped past him into the room. A blue quilt his mother had made covered the bed, and a small cot was pushed up against the wall. Lucy sat Eileen on the bed and slipped the little girl out of her dress and into her nightgown.

Caleb watched her practiced movements. She acted like a mother. He took a step closer and lowered his voice. "I know what you're up to, so you might as well give up now."

Lucy turned an anguished white face up toward him. "I don't think you do, Mr. Stanton."

"I've seen your kind blow through here before. You're just out for all the money you can bleed out of Pa, but you'll have to go through me first," he said through gritted teeth. "So why don't you just pack your things and get out before you get hurt?"

Lucy smiled wearily. "It's a bit late for that," she said softly.

"You can't mean you actually *care* for Pa," he said derisively. "He's an old man."

"It's not what you think," she said.

"Oh, I think it is." He spun around and stormed out of the room. He hadn't handled that well. She'd stayed too calm, as if she knew something he didn't. Had Pa already given her money?

Moments later, Lucy joined them in the parlor. Caleb stood staring morosely out the window at the driving snow. He turned when she entered the room and glared at her. He thought he saw tears shimmering on the tips of her lashes, but told himself he was imagining it. She was much too calculating to cry.

Luther rubbed his hands together. "Ah, Caleb, I guess I've got some explaining to do."

Caleb gave him an ironic smile. "I reckon so, Pa."

Pa stared at him with a steady gaze and a hint of compassion in his eyes. "This is Lucy, your wife."

two

Caleb's face wavered through the tears that rimmed Lucy's eyes. She had felt a thrill of joy at her first sight of her handsome husband, so strong, so manly, his feet planted apart like the king of his realm here in Texas. But with his rejection of her, all those hopeful wonderings had vanished like yesterday's sunshine.

"You mean, *your* wife," Caleb corrected. But his lips went white, and Lucy saw the shocked comprehension settle over his face.

Mr. Stanton shook his head. "No, Son, I mean *your* wife. It's time you settled down and saw to raising a family. I won't be around to help you forever. You need a passel of strong sons to begin to build our cattle empire."

Caleb sat heavily on the sofa, and the lines deepened in his tanned face. "Pa, what have you done?" he whispered.

Mr. Stanton hunched his shoulders and raised his voice defensively. "If I waited for you to find a wife, I'd be too old to enjoy my grandchildren. Lucy here, she's a good Christian girl. She'll make you a fine wife."

Lucy saw the shudder that passed through Caleb's frame. A lump grew in her throat. Did he find her so unattractive? She knew she had no claim to great beauty, but he had barely glanced her way to even know what she looked like.

Caleb waved a hand in her direction. "Look at her, Pa! What were you thinking? Any sons she bears will likely be

19

as small and spindly as she is. The work here is hard. The vision we've talked about will take a woman who can carry her own weight."

Small? Spindly? Lucy's tears dried up with the bolt of rage that shot through her. She drew herself up to her full height of just under five feet and glared at her new husband. "I'm stronger than I look, Mr. Stanton. I've worked long hours at the millinery shop, and I'm not afraid of hard work. I can tackle any chores you care to throw my way!"

She was wasting her breath; he was determined not to give her a chance. She could see it in the hard line of his jaw and the fierce glare in his eyes. But something inside her screamed to be allowed to prove her worth.

His eyes widened, and his jaw dropped. "You aren't staying long enough to find out, Miss Marsh. I aim to put you on the first stage back east."

"We *are* married," she reminded him. "I don't believe in divorce." She glared at him. He would not send her away; she had a brother and sister to care for. Her appearance might disgust him, but marriage was more than physical appearance. She would prove herself to him.

Another shudder passed through his frame. He took a deep breath. "Neither do I," he said. "But this is no real marriage. I never agreed to any such arrangement. You should have known better, Pa."

"For once in your life, listen to me, Caleb! This ranch needs a woman's touch. *You* need a woman to soften you before you turn to granite. If we're going to build a cattle empire in this place, we need sons. Strong sons. Lucy has the grit to raise sons you'll be proud of. You don't really know her yet."

"If you want a woman around the house so bad, *you* marry her," Caleb shot back.

Mr. Stanton opened his mouth to reply, then his face turned red and darkened to nearly purple. He gasped, then clutched his left shoulder. The color drained from his face, and a gargle escaped from his open mouth.

"Pa?" Caleb's voice rose, and he jumped to his feet and rushed toward his father. Luther Stanton gasped, then reeled away, crashing to the floor like a great tree felled by a logger's axe.

Lucy bit back a shriek and ran toward her new father-in-law. Caleb arrived at his father's side first. He rolled Luther over onto his back and peered into his face. The older man was still breathing, but his pallor was pronounced, and he was unconscious.

"Let me," Lucy said, pushing her way closer to Luther. "I know something of nursing."

Caleb clenched his jaw. "If he dies, his blood will be on your head. He was just fine until you came along."

Lucy ignored him. "Is there a doctor in the area?"

Caleb nodded. "Doc Cooper in Wichita Falls."

"Send Percy to fetch him, and you help me get him into bed." She checked his breathing and was relieved to see a bit of color coming back to his face. Snatching a quilted throw from the chair, she tucked it around Luther.

Bellowing for Percy, Caleb's voice echoed down the hall as he ran to do what she said. Lucy pressed her fingertips against her father-in-law's chest and frowned when she felt Luther's irregular heartbeat. He'd had some kind of a heart spasm. Her heart sank, and she was ashamed to admit that her first thoughts were of her own situation. If this man died, she would be at the mercy of her new husband. "Please God, please keep him alive," she whispered.

Caleb returned and lifted his father's shoulders. "Grab his feet," he ordered.

Lucy grabbed Luther's feet, and Jed jumped in to assist as well. They carried him up the stairs.

"His room is the first on the left," Caleb gasped. Lucy pushed open the door with her foot, and they laid Luther on the bed. Caleb jerked his father's boots off. Lucy pulled the quilts up around him.

"We need to keep him warm," she told Caleb. "His color looks bad."

Caleb nodded, then ran his hand through his sandy blond hair. His gray eyes held a deep fear that brought a hint of sympathy to Lucy's heart. She laid a hand on his arm. "We should pray for him," she said.

He nodded and moved so her hand fell away. She couldn't help the stab of disappointment at his rejection of her comfort. Suddenly aware that Jed and Eileen hovered at the doorway, she straightened her shoulders and moved away from Caleb. She had to be strong for the children's sakes. "I'll fix us all some tea," she said.

"No thanks," Caleb said. "I can't abide that sissy drink, and I'm not about to start drinking it now."

Hot words bubbled to her lips, but she choked them back. No wonder Luther had to find a wife for his son. No woman in her right mind would choose to put up with him.

Luther stirred, and his eyes fluttered open. "Quit your wrangling," he said in a weak voice. "I can't endure petty quarreling." He struggled to sit up. "Besides, the sight of Caleb sipping tea like a woman would finish me off for sure. Fetch me some coffee. That's all I need." A hint of color was returning to his face.

"I'll just be a moment," Lucy said. Away from her new husband's stern presence, she felt reprieved. She hurried down the stairs to the kitchen, with Jed and Eileen on her heels.

"I don't like it here, Lucy," Jed whispered once they were out of earshot. "I want to go back to Boston."

Eileen began to cry, and Lucy scooped her up into her arms. "Hush, Darling, it will be all right. There's flour for biscuits and beefsteak for dinner. That's more than we had in Boston. I know it's going to be an adjustment, but let's wait and see how things are tomorrow. We're all at sixes and sevens with Mr. Stanton's illness and the long trip. God hasn't brought us this far to let us down."

Jed crossed his arms and glowered at her. "Caleb acts like this was all your fault. I'd like to slug him."

"Jed, that's not respectful to your elders." She wanted to remind him that if it weren't for his foolishness, they would not be here, but she bit the words back. Recriminations would serve no purpose now.

"Caleb is just shocked at what his father has done," Lucy said. She hoped that was true. She was willing to give Caleb the benefit of the doubt, but her charity was growing thin. The thought of their single room in the boarding-house, rude though it might be, filled her with a sense of nostalgia and longing. Not that it was there anyway. It had probably already been razed into a pile of rubble.

Lucy put Eileen down and went to the stove. Wrinkling her nose at the strong smell, she poured the black coffee into a cup. Taking a sip, she shuddered at the bitterness. A sugar container was on the table, so she took it, then dumped some sugar in it and stirred it.

Sugar. What a luxury. There seemed to be plenty, too. She dipped her finger into the coffee and tasted it. Shivering at the still-bitter taste, she added more sugar, then poured another cup for Caleb and added sugar to that cup, too. At least it might be drinkable now. From the strong, acrid taste, it must have been made this morning. There was no time to make more now, though.

She carried the coffee back to Luther's bedroom. Luther was sitting up against the pillows. Though he looked wan and weak, his eyes were not so dull. He took the coffee eagerly, and she handed the other cup to Caleb. Both men took a big gulp. Caleb's eyes widened, and he choked but managed to keep it down. His father was not so charitable. Sputtering, Luther spewed the coffee from his mouth. The dark liquid pooled on the quilt in front of him.

The eyes he turned to Lucy were full of reproach and betrayal. Luther shuddered. "Sugar! You put sugar in my coffee?"

"I'm sorry." Lucy took a step back toward the door. "It was bitter."

Caleb wiped his mouth. "It's supposed to be bitter!" He took the cup from his father and brushed by Lucy on his way to the door. "Pa, I told you no good would come of having a woman around," he growled. "She's too little to be of any use on the ranch, she doesn't know coffee from syrup, and she's bound to nag us both to death. We've gotten along just fine, the two of us."

Luther scowled. "That's enough, Caleb. Lucy is your wife, and the sooner you adjust to that fact, the better. You were too young to remember what a different place this house was with your mama here, God rest her soul. We need her, try to remember that."

"She's not my wife, Pa! I never gave you permission to bring me back a bride."

"You signed a proxy statement, Caleb. It's all legal, and you'd best make the most of it."

The two men glared at one another, and Lucy thought they looked like two roosters squaring off for a fight. She should douse them both with cold water. If she had the nerve, she would. They deserved it. Luther for bringing her here without telling her his son hated women, and Caleb for not giving her a chance to prove herself. Well, she would show them! She wasn't afraid of hard work, and when Caleb realized it, his apology would be sweet.

Still lost in a pleasant daydream of Caleb groveling at her feet, she didn't notice Luther's gray color until he choked. Sinking weakly back against the pillows, he clutched his left arm again. Lucy started to his side, but Caleb beat her to it.

"Pa!" Caleb hurtled forward and crouched at his father's bedside.

Drops of perspiration beaded Luther's face. "Quit fussing," he muttered. He rallied a bit and clutched his son's hand. "Promise me you'll try to care for your new wife, Son," he whispered. "I would turn over in my grave if I thought I'd done anything to harm her and those children."

"You're not going to die, Pa!"

Luther tried to raise in the bed. "Promise me!"

Caleb stilled, and his shoulders slumped. "I promise." He shot a dark glance toward Lucy as if it were her fault his father was so truculent.

"I want her and the children to move in with you," Luther said. "I'm not sure the noise would be good for the old ticker." His voice was weak, but the odd gleam in his eye made Lucy wonder if he was using the situation to his own advantage. "Once I'm well, we'll see about getting you a decent house for a family."

Caleb's brows drew together, but he bowed his head and nodded. "Whatever you want, Pa." But the look from his gray eyes as he turned toward Lucy was anything but meek.

The time ticked by slowly. When Lucy had finally begun to wonder what had become of the doctor, he came bustling in. A stringy man with grizzled hair, Doc Cooper reminded Lucy of a miner rather than a doctor.

"What's this nonsense, Luther? You're too ornery to die on us. Let's take a look at you." Dr. Cooper jerked his head at Caleb, Lucy, and the children, and they obeyed the silent admonition to leave him alone with Luther.

In the hall, Caleb crossed his arms and leaned against the wall. "I have to hand it to you, Miss Marsh—"

"Mrs. Stanton," she corrected, unable to stop the smile that tugged at her lips. She wanted to laugh aloud at the consternation that raced across his face. Caleb had likely never had anyone buck his will. He was a spoiled child, used to getting his own way.

Caleb straightened, his face going white as he stared at her. "You laugh now, but you won't be laughing long. Life on a ranch is not the fancy parties and teas you're used to in Boston. It's hard, smelly, and dirty. Those lily-white hands won't look so pretty in a few weeks."

Lucy found it difficult to breathe. Before she could

respond, Jed stepped between her and Caleb. His fists clenched, he thrust his face into Caleb's.

"My sister is worth two of you! Eileen and me would be in the orphanage if she hadn't found a job at the millinery and kept us all together. She's come home with her fingers bleeding from the pins. And she's small 'cause when there's not enough food, she makes sure me and Eileen eat first. Lucy may not be big, but she's all heart, Mr. Stanton. You don't deserve her!"

Lucy put a hand on her brother's arm. "Hush, Jed," she murmured. "God told me to do this, that it was His will."

Caleb gave a short bark of laughter. "I find it hard to believe the Almighty told you to agree to such a plan. I don't need a wife."

A slight smile tilted Lucy's lips. "No, you don't *want* a wife, and that's a completely different situation. God sees things we don't, Mr. Stanton. I don't believe in divorce, so we must make the best of this situation. You should respect your father enough to do that much. I haven't known Luther long, but he seems a wise man. Maybe he knows more about what you need than you do."

Caleb ran a hand through his hair, and Lucy's heart softened at the vulnerability she saw on his face. This had taken him by complete surprise. She'd had time to get used to it, but Luther's actions had left Caleb reeling. "We'd better get that coffee for your pa, or he'll take a switch to you."

Surprise flickered across Caleb's face, and he lifted one eyebrow. "Figured him out already, huh?" He stared into her eyes, then his shoulders slumped. "I guess we'd best declare a truce for now. But don't think this situation will stand, Miss Lucy. You're not up to the task of building the

Stanton cattle empire."

Lucy bit her lip and held out her hand. "Truce, Mr. Stanton. I see I shall have to prove myself to you."

Her small hand was enveloped by his large, calloused one. The contact sent a thrill of awareness through her, and she nearly jerked it away. Searching the gray depths of his eyes, she wondered if he felt the awareness she did. If he did, he hid it well.

Caleb released her hand and turned toward the kitchen. "I reckon your first lesson better be coffee. A cattleman can't live without it. It warms him up on those cold nights on the cattle drive and wakes him up after a night spent tossing on the hard ground."

Lucy followed him into the kitchen. Caleb grabbed the handle of the battered coffeepot and poured the dark liquid into a tin cup. "Sugar ruins the taste." He handed her a cup. "Take a swig."

Repressing a shudder, Lucy took the cup of coffee and raised it to her lips. She mustn't let him think she was too weak to even stand up to the taste of coffee. If learning to like the vile liquid was a necessity, then she would do it. She took a gulp of coffee, and the bitter taste nearly made her gag. Managing a smile, she lowered the cup.

"That wasn't so bad, was it?"

"Do you want the truth?" A smile tugged the corners of her lips.

"Yeah."

"It's not as bad as cutting my finger off with a dull knife, but that's about all I can say for it."

Caleb stared at her for a moment, then a laugh rumbled in his throat. Lucy's heart jumped at the sound. With his face lit with amusement, he was entirely too appealing. A dimple in one cheek and the white flash of his teeth softened the tanned planes of his face, and even his towering height and broad shoulders seemed less intimidating.

Caleb poured a cup for Jed. "Here, Boy. If you aim to be a cattleman, you'd best learn, too."

Jed took it cautiously, then sniffed it. His nose wrinkled, but he took a big swallow. His eyes widened, and he coughed. "Good," he choked.

Lucy and Caleb both burst into laughter. The moment of camaraderie warmed Lucy's aching heart. Maybe things would turn out right yet. She would trust God.

three

Lucy and her siblings on his heels, Caleb pushed open the door to his father's room. What would he do if something happened to Pa? It had been just the two of them so long, ever since he could remember. Cholera had carried off his mother when he was two, and he had only vague memories of a gentle voice singing to him and a soft lap that smelled of something sweet. Maybe Pa was right, maybe it was time for him to take a wife. But he wasn't some greenhorn who needed his father to pick out a wife for him!

His pa was sitting up in the bed, some color in his face. He smiled when he saw the cup in Caleb's hand. "Coffee, just what the doctor ordered. And Lucy's pretty face will help as well." He winked at Lucy, and Caleb heard her soft laugh.

"I don't remember ordering any such thing, Luther." Doc Cooper put his stethoscope into his black bag and closed it with a snap. "I reckon one cup won't hurt, but don't go drinking too much of it. You need to rest. I'll be back in the morning." He jerked his head, and Caleb followed him into the hallway.

"How is he, Doc?"

"I won't lie to you, Caleb. He's getting old, and his ticker is just wearing out. See that he starts to take it easy, even if it means hiring more help. And try not to get him excited or upset. I know that's not easy to do with a man as active and vital as Luther has been."

Caleb's heart squeezed with pain. "I can't lose him, Doc!"

"Death comes to all of us eventually, Caleb. Lord willing, your pa will be around a few more years, but he's got to step back and learn to enjoy life. That new wife of yours will help. Luther thinks a lot of her, and she'll make him slow down, you mark my words." Doc Cooper pulled on his coat and went toward the door. "I think he'll be fine if you follow my instructions."

Caleb walked the doctor out and stood staring at the closed door, his mind numb. He couldn't make himself believe that his pa was getting old.

A soft hand touched his, and he jumped. Turning, he stared into Lucy's anxious face. "What did the doctor say?"

"Pa's heart is weak. Doc says he needs to cut back and take it easy." He blurted out the words, but it didn't ease the pain.

Lucy's eyes filled with tears. They looked luminous, like sapphire gems. "I'll take care of him," she said.

"He's my pa. I don't need any help." He regretted his words when he saw her bite her lip. He didn't know how to act around women, which was probably the reason he was still unmarried at thirty. He'd had no lack of partners at the county dances, but he invariably said the wrong thing and ended up riding home with Pa. He swallowed hard at the realization that he was no longer unmarried. This young woman with the dazzling blond hair and luminous blue eyes was his wife. His wife. He couldn't get his mind around it.

Lucy straightened her shoulders and stared into his face. "Well, you're going to get my help, whether you want it or not, Caleb Stanton! I'm your wife, and your father is now my father. The kids and I have already learned to love him. This isn't about you. It's about your pa. Our problems can wait."

She was right. He wanted to apologize, but the words stuck in his throat. He knew so little about women. Lucy was entrancing with her golden curls and pink cheeks. Her full lips looked soft and inviting. Caleb jerked his thoughts away from that direction. His priority was to see Pa better; then he could worry about getting rid of Miss Lucy and her siblings.

The next morning Caleb went to his pa's room and found it empty. Panic made his mouth go dry. He rushed down the hall and found him in the kitchen with Jed and Lucy.

"There you are, my boy." Luther pointed to a seat across from him. "Breakfast is ready. Lucy fixed the best flapjacks I've ever feasted upon."

Caleb eased into the seat and looked at the platter of flapjacks. They did look good. His stomach rumbled, and he scowled. "How'd you get Percy to give up his kitchen?"

"He didn't give it up. He shared it." Lucy's smile seemed to brighten the sunshine flooding through the window. "He fixed the coffee and eggs and let me do the flapjacks."

Truly, Lucy was a miracle worker. Percy guarded his kitchen like a dragon guarded gold. Caleb transferred a heap of flapjacks to his plate and spread jam on them. The flapjacks were light as thistledown, and Caleb dug in with gusto. "I'll say one thing," he muttered. "You sure can cook." He aimed a glance at his pa. "You're looking better, Pa."

"I feel fine. Dr. Cooper is an old woman. I aim to rest up

another day, then get out to the barn and shoe the horses."

Caleb saw Lucy open her mouth, but he shot her a look of warning, and she quickly closed it. Arguing with Pa would do no good. "Good idea," he said with a shrug. "But don't you reckon it would be bad manners to leave Lucy alone all day?"

"You're probably right. You get your chores done, then get back in here to entertain her," Luther said.

He gave a sly grin, and Caleb had to grit his teeth to keep from spewing his thoughts out. He still hadn't changed his mind over Pa's fool-headed scheme to marry him off to this pale lily of a girl. When she saw the cabin, she'd soon be hightailing it back to Massachusetts.

"I'll take her to the cabin when I get done with chores."

"I was going to suggest that," Luther said. "Lucy here is eager to see her new home."

"She may change her mind when she sees it."

"Now don't you go scaring her, Caleb. That place just needs a woman's touch. It's what your ma and I had when we were first married. You'll build her something better soon."

"It's fine like it is, but if she's expecting something like Boston, she's in for a shock."

"You needn't discuss me as though I'm not here," Lucy said.

Caleb felt a shaft of grudging respect. She knew how to hold her own.

"Can we ride a horse there?" Jed shot to his feet and practically pranced around his chair.

Caleb aimed a glance at Lucy. "Can you ride?"

"A little."

A little. A tenderfoot, just as he suspected. He shrugged and got to his feet. "Wanda is real gentle; you'll be okay on her. And Jed can ride Buck. I'll put Eileen in front of me."

Lucy stood and began to clear the dishes. "By the time you get the chores done, I'll have these dishes cleared away and Eileen fed and dressed."

"Let Percy see to those dishes. You young 'uns run along." Luther waved a hand. "You need to start settling into your new life."

His new life. Caleb slanted a glance toward Lucy. Maybe once he got used to it, the idea might not be so bad. If he just hadn't been dragged to it like a roped calf.

❧

An hour later Lucy watched the play of emotions across her new husband's face. One minute she thought he might be warming up to her, and the next, he pulled away again. If he ever loved a woman with the fierce loyalty he showed his pa, she would be a lucky woman.

"I really should help Percy," she told Caleb as she followed him from the kitchen.

"Pa won't rest until he knows we're on our way. So we'd best get it over with, then check back and see how he's doing."

Lucy nodded and fetched her bag. Jed carried his belongings, and Caleb hoisted Eileen's case to his shoulder. The snow nearly blinded her when she stepped outside.

"I hadn't been expecting snow," she told him.

"Don't get much," Caleb said. "I don't remember ever having this much. A skiff of snow is about all we ever see." He strapped the luggage to the back of a mule, then led Lucy toward a black and white horse whose markings reminded Lucy of a cow. Its forlorn stance with its shaggy back to the wind softened her heart.

"This is Wanda. Riding her is like sitting in your mama's rocking chair. She won't let you fall." The horse nuzzled Caleb's hand, and he laughed, then dug his hand into his pocket and pulled out a lump of sugar for the mare. The mare nuzzled it with soft lips from his hand.

Lucy's trepidation eased. Wanda glanced at her with gentle brown eyes, then dropped her head again. Lucy let Caleb help her into the saddle. He'd had the foresight to saddle her with a lady's sidesaddle. It was old but well oiled and in good condition. This high up, she could see out across the land. Stanton land. And she was as much a possession of Caleb's as these boundless acres. In that moment the thought terrified her.

Jed bounded onto his horse, a small buckskin that shied nervously at Jed's exuberance. Caleb lifted Eileen in his arms and showed her how to pet his horse. "This is Maxi, Eileen. Would you like to give him a lump of sugar?"

Eileen's face was white with fright, but she nodded, and Caleb gave her a lump of sugar. The gelding's lips closed gently around the sugar, and Eileen gave a squeal of delight. "I feeded the horse, Lucy!"

Lucy gave her an encouraging smile, full of pride. "You're a brave girl, Eileen," she said. So he was good with kids. That was a mark in his favor, but he had a lot of black marks to overcome.

Caleb set Eileen at the front of his saddle, then swung up behind her. "Follow me," he told Lucy and Jed.

Clutching the reins, Lucy managed to get her horse to follow Caleb's lead, but she had a sneaking suspicion it had more to do with her mare's determination not to be left behind. As the horses labored through the snowdrifts, Lucy kept stealing glances at Caleb's firm jaw. She had so many questions she wanted to ask him, but her tongue seemed stuck to the roof of her mouth.

They traveled over a hill, and she saw a frozen creek in the valley below. A building crouched beside it, the siding gray and worn. A small, leafless tree, shaking in the wind, seemed to cower under the small house for cover.

Lucy smiled. The way he'd talked, she was imagining a soddy or something even worse. He didn't know how rude their former lodgings were. This little place was simply waiting for her. Its forlorn appearance warmed her with the desire to make a difference. This would be home, and she would make Caleb glad his father had found her. She would earn his admiration and respect yet.

Caleb pulled his horse to a halt and jumped down, then pulled Eileen down against his chest. His gaze scanned Lucy's face, and puzzlement clouded his face when she gave him a serene smile.

"It's not much," he said. There seemed to be regret in his voice, and Lucy wondered if he was ashamed of the little cabin.

Her smile warmed. "It's charming."

His eyes widened, and he gave her a sharp look, then turned to go inside.

Jed dismounted and thrust his hands into his pockets. Surveying the small shanty, he turned to Caleb with a grin. "This doesn't look so bad, Mr. Stanton. Lucy's real good at fixing stuff up. You should see the apartment we used to live in."

Lucy felt the heat of a blush on her cheeks. Such faith was humbling. Her gaze was drawn to the cabin again. It seemed to call her like a long-lost child. In her mind's eye, she could see a small garden patch out front and wild roses climbing on a trellis under the kitchen window where she could enjoy the fragrance.

Eileen sidled closer to Lucy and thrust her small hand into Lucy's larger one. "I have to go potty, Lucy," she whispered.

Caleb's expression softened. "Outhouse is out back," he said. "I'll show you, Eileen."

The little girl shrank back and put her thumb in her mouth. Her blue eyes sought her sister's face. "I want Lucy," she whispered.

Caleb nodded. "Let's get inside, and then you can go out the back door instead of traipsing through the snow."

His voice was gentle when he spoke to Eileen. Studying him, Lucy thought he might make a good father once he lost that gruff exterior. He wasn't nearly as hard as he tried to convince everyone he was. She followed him into the cabin and looked around.

Her first impression was of dark, dingy wood and dust. The floor was unpainted plank. It needed a good cleaning more than anything else. A hastily constructed table and a single chair were shoved against the wall by the wood stove. A wood box beside the stove was heaped with kindling that had spilled over onto the floor.

She walked to the kitchen. The stove needed scrubbing and several dirty plates and cups sat in a dishpan on the dry sink. She shivered, not so much from the temperature as from the coldness of the room's atmosphere. But she would fix that.

"I know there aren't enough chairs, but I wasn't expecting company." Caleb pulled the single chair out from the table and nodded toward it. "Have a seat."

"I need to take Eileen out back," she said. Without waiting for a reply, she took Eileen's hand and quickly stepped to the back door. The privy was sturdy and well made. While she waited for Eileen, Lucy glanced at the back of the cabin. It was well constructed, too. She thought he seemed competent in whatever he decided to put his hand to.

Eileen came from the privy, and Lucy took her hand and led her back inside. She found Caleb poking at the fire in the stove while Jed handed him kindling. Heat was already beginning to ease the chill of the room.

"Good, I'll need hot water for my work," Lucy said.

"Work? There won't be anything to do today. The cattle have been fed, and I'll take Jed out with me to break the ice for them to water. You and Eileen can stay inside and keep warm."

Lucy waved a hand. "Look at this place. We can't sleep in this filth."

Caleb's brows drew together. "Filth?" His voice went up at the end of the word. "There's nothing wrong with my cabin. It's not the fanciest home in the Red River Valley, but it would suit any other woman who was used to homesteading. But I knew a city girl like you would turn your nose up at it."

Lucy refused to let him rile her. "The accommodations are fine, Caleb. It's the lack of cleanliness I object to. Now you and Jed just run along. We're going to need some beds, too. See what you can do. When you get back, you'll see how much better it looks with a woman's touch."

Caleb's mouth hung open, and he just stared at her.

"I wouldn't argue with her, Mr. Stanton," Jed said.

Lucy didn't wait to see if Caleb would take Jed's advice. Taking Eileen by the hand, she grabbed a bucket and headed for the door. "I'll need some water for scrubbing."

"I'll get it." Caleb roused from his stupor and snatched the pail from her. "The pump is out back, but it might be hard to start. I haven't used it for a few days. Just stay put and don't touch anything."

Lucy nearly smiled at the alarm in his voice. Caleb now had a family to look out for, and he seemed to be taking the responsibility seriously. Jed followed him out the door. Putting her hands on her hips, Lucy turned and surveyed the room. They could put some beds against the west wall and there was space for some extra chairs by the fire. The loft overhead was empty. It would serve as the main bedroom.

Heat scorched her cheeks at the thought of sharing a room with Caleb. Not yet, she prayed. She wasn't ready yet. It was a blessing from God that Caleb was so uncertain about the marriage. Time would help them both to adjust to the thought that they were tied for life.

She found an apron in her bag and tied it on. "Eileen, would you like to help me?"

The little girl nodded. "I can do the dishes."

"All right. As soon as Mr. Stanton gets back with the water, I'll heat some, and you can wash up." Lucy looked around again. There wasn't even a broom! No wonder the place needed a woman's touch.

The front door blew open, and Caleb and Jed stumbled inside with the scent of moisture and a blast of cold air. Stomping the snow from his feet, Caleb carried a bucket of water to her. "Where do you want it?"

"There by the stove. Do you have a pan to heat it in? And I need a broom."

"A broom?" Caleb said the words as if he'd never heard of a broom before. He looked around the room as if a broom might materialize from the mere thought.

"I need to sweep."

"It's just a rough plank floor. Sweeping won't do any good."

"Even a plank floor can be kept clean, Mr. Stanton."

His bewildered expression deepened. "But why? You just walk on it. It's not like it's fine hardwood or carpet."

The corner of Lucy's mouth turned up, and she bit her tongue to keep from laughing. The poor man had no clue. "Just find me a broom, and you'll see what I mean."

Caleb scowled. "Let's go, Jed. There's no pleasing a woman."

"I'll be very pleased with a broom," she called after them. Chuckling, she went to heat the water. By the time the water was hot, Caleb was back with a makeshift broom of straw.

When he gave it to her, she handed him the bucket again. "I need more water."

He rolled his eyes but didn't protest. Jed giggled. "I think you're getting domesticated, Mr. Stanton."

Caleb widened his eyes. "I'm just doing what needs done for my own protection, Jed. Your sister may be small, but she's determined." He dropped the bucket and swung Eileen into his arms. "Hey, Sweetheart, there's a new calf in the barn, you want to see?"

Eileen squealed with delight. "Can I pet it?"

"He might suck your fingers."

Eileen looked doubtfully at her hand, then turned her sunny smile back to Caleb. "I don't mind."

"Okay, get your coat."

"Can I come, too?" Lucy asked. The thought of a new calf was suddenly much more appealing than cleaning.

"Sure you can spare the time from your sweeping?" Caleb's grin clutched at her heart.

"I'll take the time."

"Just don't blame me if you have to sleep with the spiders."

Spiders? Lucy eyed the room. There *were* a great many cobwebs. "Maybe tomorrow," she said.

"The cleaning or the calf?"

"The calf," she said reluctantly.

His grin widened, and he went to the door with Eileen in his arms. "You don't know what you're missing."

Lucy was sure that was true. This was a side to Caleb she hadn't seen before. But sometimes duty was more important than fun. She had to earn her keep and show Caleb she could be the wife he needed. He would never love her unless she could prove herself.

Holding the broom like a sword, she swept through the cabin like an avenging angel. Spiders scuttled from her attack. Stomping and shouting, she killed all she could find and swept the room clean of dirt and cobwebs. When the water was hot, she washed the dishes, then used the still-warm water to scrub the floors, swirling the water around with her broom before mopping it up on her hands and knees.

She was almost afraid to check the loft; there were probably even more spiders there. With shaking knees, she climbed the ladder. Poking her head over the top, she looked around. It was as she feared. The entire loft was criss-crossed with spider webs laden with fat bodies, alive and dead. Shuddering, she backed down the ladder. There was no way she could do that herself. She would get Jed to make the first pass. Or maybe even Caleb.

Caleb. The thought of his derision was almost enough to make her go back up, but she couldn't quite make herself mount that ladder again. She should have cleaned upstairs first. Now some of those spiders would probably come down here.

Her earlier euphoria vanished. Maybe she really wasn't cut out to be a cattleman's bride. If she couldn't face up to something as small as a spider, what would she do with a bull? But the thought of a bull wasn't nearly as daunting as those plump bodies upstairs.

She looked around her new kitchen. She could at least start a meal. She went to the small pantry and opened it. Something black moved in the corner, and Lucy stared at it for a moment before it moved again. She backed away, a scream lodged in her throat. It couldn't be what it appeared. Spiders didn't grow that big or that hairy. Then it scuttled toward her, and the paralysis in her vocal chords broke. She shrieked with all the breath in her lungs and bolted for the door.

four

"He likes his nose scratched." Caleb guided Eileen's small hand to the calf's nose.

"What's his name?" Eileen scratched the calf's nose, then giggled when its mouth opened and it began to suck on her finger.

"He doesn't have one. This is a working ranch. We can't get attached to our livestock."

"Why? She's pretty." Eileen patted the calf with her small hand. "Can I call her Elsie?"

Before Caleb could explain why it wasn't a good idea to get attached to the calf, a shriek echoed from the house. Caleb jerked and knocked over a pitchfork. The scream was full of panic and terror.

"Stay here and hide!" he ordered the children. Jed instinctively grabbed his little sister and pulled her behind a feed barrel. Grabbing a shotgun by the door, Caleb pelted toward the house. The blood thundered in his ears. Just last month the Landers family had been wiped out by Indians.

Lucy screamed again, and the sound made his blood curdle. He reached the front of the house and stood for a moment collecting his wits. Maybe he should try getting in the back door. The Indians likely were watching this one. But before he could move toward the back, the front door flew open, and Lucy came stumbling out.

43

Her face was white, and her blue eyes mindless with terror. Those eyes widened when she saw him; then the next thing he knew, she was burrowing into his arms. She barely came to his chest, and still holding his rifle, he held her close. Her shoulders shook, and she made frantic little mews of panic. Holding her close, he tried to peer into the cabin as he steered her to the safety of the side yard.

"Indians?" he whispered, patting her back awkwardly.

She shook her head so hard pins flew from her hair, and golden strands fell to her shoulders. "Spider," she gasped. She shuddered again, and his arms tightened around her.

"A spider?" he asked, pushing her away.

Lucy shuddered again, returning to his grasp. "It was as big as my hand. And—and *hairy*." She burrowed deeper into his jacket.

"Probably a tarantula," he said. The corner of his mouth lifted, and he felt almost giddy with relief. His chest rumbled with the effort to hide his mirth.

Lucy lifted her head. "Are you *laughing*?"

A chuckle escaped. "It's probably Pete. He was in the pantry, right?"

Her eyes wide with horror, Lucy took a step back. "This spider *lives* there? And you *named* him?"

Caleb was surprised to find he regretted letting go of her. "Sure, he eats the bugs."

Lucy shuddered. "You have to kill it."

He shook his head. "Nope. Pete stays."

She crossed her arms. "Then I go. I'm not sharing my home with a hairy spider."

Caleb narrowed his eyes. "Fine. I didn't want you here anyway."

"I'll stay with your father until you get that, that *thing* out of there."

His father. Caleb gritted his teeth. If she went back to the big house, it might upset Pa. He would think Caleb wasn't being a proper husband. And maybe he wasn't, Caleb admitted. He would be the first to admit he had no idea of what women found important. But what gave this little woman the right to waltz into his home and start giving orders?

"I'll take Pete to the barn," he said.

"Then I won't go in the barn!"

Caleb let out an exasperated sigh and shook his head. Women. There was no pleasing them. "I thought you wanted to learn to be a proper rancher's wife. That includes helping out in the barn. And making peace with beneficial bugs like tarantulas."

"Spiders aren't insects; they're arachnid. And they're hideous." Lucy shuddered.

Tears shimmered on her lashes, and Caleb realized for the first time that she was truly terrified. This was not some power ploy. She was petrified. Backing away from him, a sob rose from her chest, and she hiccupped. Remorse smote Caleb. She would think he was a fiend.

He put a hand on her shoulder. "I'm sorry, Lucy. Pete won't hurt you."

Lucy burst into tears and covered her face with her hands. "I've been trying so hard," she sobbed. "I want to be a blessing to you, Mr. Stanton. You must think you've been saddled with some weak woman who needs pampering. Truly, I can carry my side of the bargain, but I can't abide spiders. Especially ones who need a close shave. Preferably with a very sharp blade."

Caleb suppressed his grin when she shuddered. He pulled her back into his arms. She seemed to fit there. He rested his chin on her head and breathed in the fragrance of her hair. It smelled clean with a hint of something sweet, maybe lavender. Something stirred in his heart. Whether he'd planned it or not, this woman was his wife. He might not love her, but he had to make accommodations for her in his life, even if it meant ridding the house of creepy crawlies.

He hugged her gently. "I'll get rid of Pete," he said.

She turned her wet face up to him. "You will? It won't even be in the barn?"

"I'll take him out somewhere and let him loose."

She smiled, and it was like the sun burst through the storm clouds. "Thank you, Mr. Stanton," she whispered. A shadow darkened her eyes.

"What's wrong?"

"Um, there're other spiders in the loft. Could you get rid of them, too?"

He grinned. "Those I can kill." He released her and went inside.

"I'll just stay out here until the spiders are gone," she called.

Caleb stepped inside the room and stopped short. His eyes widened. Was this the same place? It was spotless. He whistled softly through his teeth. Maybe this marriage thing wouldn't be so bad. He hadn't even noticed all the dust and cobwebs until they were gone.

He strode through the house until he found Pete crouched in a corner of the pantry. "Sorry, old friend, you have to go out into the cold." He held out his hand, and the tarantula crawled onto his sleeve. He carried the spider out the back door and walked out into the field until he couldn't see the cabin anymore, then shook Pete off into the melting snow. The spider seemed to look at him reproachfully, then scurried off toward a stand of cottonwood trees by the river.

Now for the rest of the spiders. Caleb hurried back to the cabin. Grabbing the broom, he climbed the ladder to the loft. He swatted and squashed spiders until all that was left were dead remains, then swept them all up onto a piece of tin he found. He carried them out the back door so Lucy wouldn't see them and tossed them into the field.

He was still smiling when he went looking for Lucy. She was in the barn with the children, and she jumped when he stepped through the door. Her face was still pale, but she met his gaze bravely.

"It's gone," he said. "So are the ones in the loft."

Relief flooded her face, and she gave him a tremulous smile. "Thank you, Mr. Stanton. Are you hungry?"

"Starved. Let me show you where the root cellar is. I have smoked meat down there as well as some vegetables." Taking the shovel, Caleb led the way to the back of the cabin and shoveled away the snow to reveal a cellar door. He tugged it up. "Get me the broom, and I'll make sure you don't have to deal with any unwanted guests down there, either."

She gave him a grateful smile, and he felt as tall as Paul Bunyan. They would learn to rub along together. All they needed was time.

While Lucy fixed the meal, he took the children back to the barn, where he had them help him muck out the horse stalls. Before long the aroma of beef and potatoes wafted across the yard. His mouth watered. Usually all he managed was a slice of cold smoked meat. He rarely bothered with more than that.

He tossed the pitchfork into the pile of straw. "That's it, kids. Let's go get some grub." He lifted Eileen in his arms, and they trooped toward the house. As they neared the house, he heard Lucy scream his name. "Must be another spider," he told Jed. Grinning, he set Eileen down at the front door and grabbed the broom. It sounded like it came from the backyard. Maybe Pete had found his way back.

As he rounded the corner of the house, he heard snarling. The hair on the back of his neck rose. That was no spider. It sounded like a wolf or a dog, and he'd left his rifle in the barn. He heard a whimper from Lucy and broke into a run.

A large mongrel, half wolf, half dog, blocked Lucy's way to the house. A twig clutched in her hand, she stood with her back pressed to the outhouse. Caleb raised the broom like a club, but before he could swing it, the animal launched itself at Lucy's throat. Caleb let out an involuntary cry, then a golden shape came hurtling across the yard and crashed into the mongrel in midair. Mongrel and dog rolled over together, both snarling and growling. Fur flew like blowing snow. The ruckus brought the two children to the back door.

"Get back inside!" Lucy shouted. She eased away from the outhouse and ran to Caleb. "Do something," she panted. "It will kill the dog."

The children stood paralyzed in the doorway. "Jed, get my rifle!"

The boy nodded and shut the door. Caleb propelled Lucy toward the door. "I'll handle this. You get inside." He opened the door and pushed her inside.

Her eyes pleading and frantic, she stood in the doorway. "That dog saved my life. You can't let that—that wolf or whatever it is—kill him."

She was right. He nodded and turned with the broom. When he whacked the mongrel wolf across the head, it turned toward him, its jaws open in a snarl. It lunged at him, but the dog renewed the attack and seized the wolf by the back leg. They rolled together again, snarling and spitting.

Caleb brought the broom down on the mongrel wolf's head with all his might, and the broom handle broke. The wolf yelped and shook the dog off, then launched itself at Caleb.

A gun boomed, and the mongrel fell at Caleb's feet. Stunned both by the suddenness of the attack and the loud crack of the rifle, he stood there a moment with the snow turning to crimson at his feet. The air was acrid with the scent of gunpowder. Turning his head, he found Lucy holding the smoking rifle.

Lucy dropped the rifle and ran into the yard to the dog. It was a golden retriever. The dog's ribs showed through its mangy, bloodied coat, and it licked her hand when she knelt beside it.

Lucy turned a pleading gaze to Caleb. "Can you help the poor thing?"

Caleb knelt beside her and ran gentle hands over the dog. It whimpered when he touched its wounds but made no move to bite him. "Good girl," he soothed. He scooped the dog up in his arms and stood. "Let's get her inside."

Lucy held the door open, and he carried the dog inside and laid her down by the fire. "I need some hot water and old rags. There should be some in the pantry."

Lucy hurried to find what he needed while he opened his toolbox and found some scissors. He cut away as much of the fur as he could and winced at the deep bites and lacerations on the dog. He washed the wounds with the water and rags Lucy provided, then bandaged the worst of the bites on the dog's leg.

"How'd you learn to shoot like that?" He felt a curious mixture of pride and curiosity.

"Lucy can shoot a walnut out of a tree," Jed said with obvious pride. "Pa said she took to hunting and shooting like most women take to meddling."

Caleb's mouth lifted in a smile. "Sounds like your pa had some bad experience with women."

Lucy flushed. "He liked to tease Mama. She was always helping out the neighbors. Pa called it meddling, but he was really very proud of her. She showed Christ's love wherever and whenever she could."

"I never knew my ma," Caleb said. "I was only two when she died, and all I remember is the scent of her hair and her soft lap." He regretted the words as soon as he saw Lucy's face soften. He didn't want pity. She'd already saved him from the mongrel wolf; he didn't want her to unman him anymore.

He stood. "She should be all right. We'll keep her inside until she's well enough to turn outside again."

"Can I keep her?" Eileen asked. Her small hands patted the dog's head, and the dog licked the little girl's fingers feebly.

Caleb hesitated. "I reckon so. I don't have a dog right now, since Rolf died last fall. This lady doesn't look like she belongs to anyone; she's much too thin. But we should put out in Wichita Falls we've got her. She looks to be a valuable animal."

Eileen's face clouded. "She's mine. No one else can have her."

Lucy patted Eileen's head. "I doubt anyone will claim her. What are you going to name her?"

Eileen kept patting her head. "What would be a good name for such a brave doggy?"

"How about Bridget? It's Irish for strong." Lucy put a bowl of water near the dog.

"Good girl, Bridget," Eileen crooned, patting the dog again. Bridget thumped her tail on the floor, and Eileen flung her arms around Bridget's neck.

"Looks like she approves," Caleb said. "Now if we're all finished with the dog, can we eat? My stomach is gnawing on my backbone."

Lucy's lips curved in a smile, and he found himself fascinated with the way her teeth gleamed and the smooth pink of her cheeks. He shook himself out of his reverie. A lucky shot with the rifle wasn't enough to get past his guard. He would bide his time and see where her true character lay.

After the meal, Lucy put Eileen down for a nap on a mat beside Bridget. Caleb took Jed and went outside to bury the mongrel wolf and to knock together some beds in the barn. He had Jed take some feed sacks in to Lucy to stitch together for mattress covers. They built two beds, one for Lucy and Eileen and one for Jed. Lucy was beautiful, but he knew it was much too soon for her to share a bed with him, even if he wished it. And he didn't. Not yet. She had shown some courage today, but she still wasn't the wife he'd envisioned for himself. It would take more than a pretty face and a good meal to win him over.

As if the thought had brought her, Lucy stepped into the barn with the feedbags over her arm. "Eileen is still sleeping. Could I get some straw to stuff the mattresses?"

Caleb pointed to the stack of clean straw at the back of the barn. "Help yourself."

He watched her kneel and begin to stuff the bags full of straw. A shaft of sunlight shone through a crack in the barn siding and lit her hair with gold. He dragged his glance away. Pa would be smirking at the easy way he was letting his defenses down.

"We've got the beds done," he said, standing to his feet.

"Are we staying here tonight?"

"I want to check on Pa, but we'll come back here afterwards. That's what he wants, and Doc says we need to humor him."

Her cheeks pink from exertion, she turned to face him. "There are many things we need to set up a home. Would your pa have extra he could share?"

Caleb stiffened. "I'm no pauper, Lucy. Give me a list of what you need, and I'll get it in Wichita Falls."

She inclined her neck. "I would like to go with you, if I might."

Great. Now the whole town would gawk at her like she was his prize filly. He shrugged. "Suit yourself. When Eileen wakes up, we'll go see Pa, then take a quick run to town." He hefted an end of the bed and nodded for Jed to pick up the other end. Carrying the bed to the house, he reflected on how the day had turned out nothing like he expected.

five

Lucy wanted to sit in the corner and wail like a baby. Discouragement slowed her steps as she trudged after Caleb to the barn. Not only had she gone into hysterics over a spider, but she had let a mongrel corner her. Why hadn't she faced the animal down and forced it to back off? Instead, she had acted like a damsel in distress. What would Caleb think?

Mounting her horse, she glanced at Caleb from the corner of her eye. He didn't seem to be upset by her failure. But he had to be wondering if she was entirely too frightened and sissified to be of much use on the ranch. The Triple S would never take its place with the big cattle empires with her slowing him down.

Caleb was a fine man, and he deserved a strong wife, one who faced up to the challenges of this wild land instead of screaming for help over a spider a fraction of her size. She wished she could get over her fear of spiders, but it had dogged her ever since she could remember. A warm feeling enveloped her when she remembered the way he'd taken care of the spiders and faced up to the mongrel.

"Will Bridget be all right?" Eileen asked. Her blue eyes were enormous in her pale face as she peered around Caleb from her perch in front of him. It had been a hard day for such a little girl. She'd never gotten a full nap, and the terror of the mongrel wolf had taken its toll on them all.

All except Caleb. His face tanned and strong, he rode easy in his saddle, his knees hugging the horse as though it was an extension of himself. His sandy hair blew in the wind, and his gray eyes looked luminous in the sun. He was a man a woman could depend on. Lucy had learned that much already. Not many men would have displayed his sense of humor over her fear of spiders. And he hadn't hesitated to rush to defend her from the mongrel.

No other man, and a stranger at that, had ever offered to protect her before. The warmth she felt toward Caleb for that unconscious gesture baffled Lucy. She'd always prided herself on taking care of everyone else, yet her deepest being longed for someone like Caleb to nurture and protect her. How could she earn his love if she wasn't all he wanted in a wife? She would have to work harder.

She realized she hadn't answered Eileen. "The dog will be fine, Sweetheart. I left her water and some food. We'll be back in a few hours."

In a few hours it would be bedtime. Lucy's mouth went dry at the thought of the coming night. She'd fixed Caleb's bed in the loft, but what would she do if he expected her to join him there? She would just have to tell him the children needed her close for awhile. And it was the truth. But he seemed too aloof to expect her company in bed.

They rounded the bend in the road, and the ranch house came into view. It felt like home to Lucy already. The two-story house sprawled in several directions, and the front porch beckoned her like an old friend. Over the crest of the hill, she could see several riders rounding up cattle, and Lucy straightened in her saddle. Craning her neck, she wished she could go watch them, but there was no time today. But someday, she promised herself, she would learn just what cowboys did.

Caleb stopped at the barn and dismounted, then pulled Eileen down. He tossed his reins to a ranch hand, then stepped over to help Lucy. She lost her balance when she slid out of the saddle, but he caught her before she could tumble to the ground. Pressed against his hard chest, she caught the aroma of the bay rum he'd used to wash his hair. The pleasant, masculine scent, combined with his proximity, brought the heat to her cheeks.

His gray eyes lingered on her lips while his hands spanned her waist. Lucy had never been this close to a man before, with the exception of her father. Looking deep into his eyes, she felt a connection she'd never felt. In spite of his casual manner, her nearness affected him more than she'd realized. She stepped away and put a trembling hand to her hair to make sure it was still in place.

Caleb's hand dropped, and Eileen took it as though he had put it down for her. Caleb exchanged an amused grin with Lucy.

"Watch it or she'll have you wrapped around her little finger," Lucy whispered.

"Too late," Caleb whispered back. "I was lost when she let the calf suck her fingers. She has a lot of spirit like her sister." He looked away. "I never did say thank you for your sharp-shooting."

Heat scorched Lucy's cheeks again. "It was the least I could do for making you give up your pet." A slight shudder passed through her frame.

"You replaced Pete with Bridget."

"At least Bridget looks good with hair."

Caleb grinned. "Pete would be offended that you didn't care for his haircut."

"He's lucky I didn't have my way. If I had, he would have been bald and flattened."

Caleb chuckled. He opened his mouth, but the door swung open, and Doc Cooper let himself out. His lean face held a trace of worry, and Lucy tensed with concern.

The mirth left Caleb's face as well, and he reached out to touch the doctor's arm. "How's Pa?"

Doc pressed his lips together. "Weaker than I'd like to see him. He had another spell a few hours ago."

Caleb's face went white. "I should have been here."

"No, no, Percy fetched me, and your pa is resting comfortably."

"We'd better stay here instead of at my place."

Doc nodded. "Couldn't hurt. That's providing the old coot will let you coddle him a bit. I'm not telling you anything you don't know when I say your pa is the most stubborn man I know."

A ghost of a smile lifted one corner of Caleb's mouth. "He's ornerier than a newly branded calf when he's sick. I'm not sure my—my wife is up to this."

The doctor's eyebrows went up to his hairline. "I wondered who this pretty lady was, Caleb. Where you been hiding her?" He turned to Lucy and nodded. "These two cowpokes have needed a woman's hand for a long time. It's a big job, though, Missus. I'll be praying for you to withstand the strain."

Lucy laughed and took hold of his hand. "Until you've faced matrons determined to fit into clothes two sizes to small for them, you don't know what strain is, Dr. Cooper.

I think I can handle two cantankerous men. But the prayers would be most welcome."

The doctor guffawed and slapped his hat on his leg. "You've got your work cut out for you handling this little woman, Caleb. I wish I could be a fly on the wall and watch." Still grinning, he went toward his buckboard. "Call me if you need me," he said before climbing into the seat.

Lucy's face burned. Sneaking a peek at Caleb, she caught his stare fixed on her with an expression on his face she couldn't read. "I'm sorry, Mr. Stanton, I didn't mean to cause you embarrassment," she whispered. "When will I ever learn to watch my tongue?"

"I thought you handled yourself right well. Doc's sense of humor can be pretty intimidating. I was proud of you."

A lump grew in Lucy's throat. He was proud of her! No one had ever told her that. Her parents were stern disciplinarians and were stingy with their praise. And for three years now, her life had been consumed with the thankless task of putting enough food on the table for her brother and sister. Caleb's pride, for she recognized that emotion on his face now, was heady stuff.

She struggled to answer him, but the lump grew larger not smaller, and for a moment she was afraid she would cry. Then Caleb pushed open the door and motioned for her to go in. The aroma of beef and potatoes and the warmth of the fire welcomed them. Caleb strode straight toward the hall to the bedrooms. Lucy and the children trailed behind him.

Before they reached Luther's bedroom, they could hear his voice raised in disgust. "Look at this food, Percy, it's not fit for man nor beast. Bring me some of that stew I smell cooking. A man needs more than this thin broth! I'll waste away to nothing."

"Doc Cooper thinks you need to shed a few pounds, Boss. This is good for you. He told me not to let you have none of that stew just yet," Percy said.

Lucy crowded behind Caleb to peer into the bedroom. Luther turned his head and saw them at the door. "Give me that spoon." He snatched it from Percy's hand. "I'm not so far gone I can't feed myself. Get in here, all of you; don't stand there gawking.

Lucy followed Caleb into the room and went to the bed. "Can I help you, Mr. Stanton?"

He waved a hand. "I've had all I can take of Doc and Percy treating me like an old woman. Tell me about your day. How do you like your new home?"

What could she say? That it was better than she'd ever imagined herself mistress of? That much was true. But she'd always imagined sharing a home with a man who loved her, not some stranger, kind though he had been today.

"I didn't get much of a chance to see it until I cleaned it," she said. "Your son is not the best housekeeper."

Caleb pulled up a chair and propped a booted leg on it. "She didn't cotton to Pete. I had to take him to the back forty and let him go." Though his tone sounded injured, the glance he sent Lucy's way was full of mirth.

"Good for her. I never did understand why you had a spider as big as a dinner plate wandering around your place."

Caleb shrugged. "Oh, and she saved my hide when she shot a mongrel wolf aimed straight at my throat."

A bit of color came back to Luther's pale face, and he

sat up a bit straighter. "I told you our Lucy would make you a fine wife, Caleb. Sometimes your old dad knows what he's doing."

Lucy saw Caleb press his lips together, and her earlier euphoria vanished. He was trying to be a good sport, but he still wished she'd never shown up with his father. Suppressing a sigh, she spent some time talking with Luther, urging him to eat his broth with a promise that he could have some more at suppertime.

When she saw Caleb stirring restlessly, she stood. "We must be going, Mr. Stanton. There are some things we need in town."

"We'll be back for the night in a few hours," Caleb said.

"I thought you were going to stay at your place," his father grumbled.

"We will when you're better."

Luther pointed a bony finger at his son. "You'll do no such thing. I won't be coddled, Caleb. When the good Lord calls me home, I'll go, but until then I intend to get on with my life and have you get on with yours. If you want to do something for me, produce me a grandchild before I die."

Caleb's nostrils flared, and Lucy dropped her gaze to the floor. Her face was hot, and she didn't dare look at Caleb again. She wanted to run from the room in mortification. Gritting her teeth, she lifted her head and mustered her strength enough to smile sweetly at her father-in-law. "We'll be going now, Mr. Stanton. We'll check in on you tomorrow."

"Do you think you could bring yourself to call me Pa or at least Luther?" the old man asked.

Lucy's heart softened. She already cared for him; how could she deny such a heartfelt request. "All right, P-Pa."

Luther's cheeks gained a bit of pink, and he relaxed against the pillows. "You're a good girl, Lucy. If I was thirty years younger, I would have married you myself. Lucky for Caleb I was too old to compete with a young buck like him." His voice trailed away, and he fell asleep, his mouth open in a soft snore.

Still churning inside from Luther's mention of children, Lucy almost flinched when Caleb touched her elbow and guided her out of the room. She found the children in the parlor and had them get their coats, all the while conscious of Caleb's overwhelming presence beside her. She longed to be back in Boston, away from these confusing emotions that ravaged her as that mongrel wolf had ravaged Bridget. The coming night terrified her. What if Caleb took his father's request seriously and demanded his husbandly rights? Swallowing hard, she threw her cloak about her shoulders and went outside.

"How about we take the buckboard to town? The snow is almost melted, and we'll need the space to bring our supplies home," Caleb asked.

"Whatever you say," Lucy said.

Caleb went to hitch the horses to the buckboard, and Lucy turned to stare out at the land. Though the day had warmed enough for the snow to melt, the air still held a crisp edge. Lucy wondered if she would still be here when spring finally came. She didn't know whether to pray for that or not. Taking her place as this man's wife, in all ways, brought the blood hammering to her face and left her trembling.

But her mama hadn't raised her to be a coward. She

drew herself up to her full height and marched toward the buckboard. Following behind her, Jed and Eileen were strangely quiet, as if they sensed her mood. Caleb tossed Eileen up onto the second seat, and Jed joined her there. Caleb's big hands spanned Lucy's waist as he lifted her to the seat. His grip held on a moment longer than necessary, and Lucy saw the same trepidation in his eyes that she felt.

Her face softened, and she yearned to touch his cheek with her fingertips, but she resisted the impulse. They had much to learn about one another, and she didn't want to rush anything.

The trip to town was silent, broken only by Eileen's chatter. Lucy tensed as the buckboard rattled nearer the cluster of buildings that was Wichita Falls. She dreaded the pleasantries she would have to face as Caleb's new wife. Just from looking at their holdings, she guessed the Stantons were a prominent cattle family.

Caleb stopped the buckboard in front of the general store. "Ready?" he asked.

"About as ready as a chicken is to get its neck wrung off," Lucy muttered.

Caleb grinned. "It won't be as bad as what you've already faced today. Come on, let me introduce you, and you can pick out everything you need." He jumped out of the wagon and held up his arms for Lucy.

He helped her down. "Jed, collect your little sister and meet us inside. You all need some new clothes, so we might as well get them while we're here."

Lucy stopped in her tracks. "I'll not have you buying us all these things, Mr. Stanton. People will say I married you for your money."

"That's pretty accurate, though, isn't it?" he asked quietly. "If you'd had enough money, you wouldn't have agreed to my father's plan. You would have found some other way around it."

Lucy's eyes stung with outraged tears, though she knew what he said was true. She *would* have spurned Luther's offer if she'd had any recourse. She would have paid whatever was necessary to get Jed out of trouble and gone on with her life in Boston.

Caleb held up a hand. "I didn't mean to insult you, Lucy. What's done is done. Now we have to see if we can work this marriage out so we're not at each other's throats like Bridget and the mongrel."

Choking back the tears, Lucy pinned a smile in place and took hold of his arm. Caleb led her into the general store, milling with people, mostly women. The familiar scents of cinnamon and mint mingled with leather and perspiration. It smelled just like the general store she frequented back in Boston, and a wave of homesickness gripped her.

The chatter in the store ceased as they stepped to the middle of the large room that was crammed with everything from food stuffs to notions to tools. Every gaze in the room pinned Lucy in her tracks. Gathering her courage, she managed to smile as Caleb introduced her.

"While you're all here, I'd like to introduce you to my wife, Lucy," he announced.

A collective gasp went around the room, and Lucy couldn't help noticing the way several women turned to look at a tall, rawboned woman standing near the glass jars of candy. Her thick red hair was caught carelessly in a tail at her neck, and she wore leather boots similar to Caleb's under her heavy skirt. Though not at all pretty, she exuded an animal magnetism that held Lucy's attention.

At Caleb's words, the woman's head snapped back as though she were slapped. Her deep green eyes, her one claim to beauty, looked almost feverish, but she was the first to offer her congratulations. Hectic spots of red in her cheeks, she held her head high as she stepped forward with an outstretched hand. "Congratulations, Lucy. You've succeeded where so many of us have lost. We thought Caleb here would die a bachelor. I'm Margaret O'Brien, your neighbor to the south."

Margaret's handshake was firm, almost like a man's. Lucy's heart sank like an anvil in water. This was the woman Caleb should have married. Lucy felt like an incompetent child next to her. No wonder Caleb was upset. This woman could have been his partner in every meaning of the word. Lucy would never manage to fill those large boots.

"Pleased to meet you," she choked.

Margaret raised her gaze to meet Caleb's. "I wish you well, Caleb," she said. Then her composure failed, and tears filled her eyes. With a muttered apology, Margaret fled the store with an almost palpable wave of sympathy behind her. Lucy felt small and mean that she had hurt this woman, even unknowingly.

Once the store door slammed, the glares from the other women should have cowed Lucy, but she couldn't let them. Too much depended on her fitting in here. She managed a smile. "I do hope you'll feel free to call on us whenever you can. I look forward to learning much about ranching from you."

Several of the women looked at one another, then one by one the women grudgingly welcomed her to the community. After a pause bordering on rudeness, they then scuttled out the door, no doubt to find Margaret and commiserate with her. And who could blame them? Lucy was an interloper here. She glanced at Caleb. He wore a bewildered smile, and she wondered how much he'd kept company with Margaret. But Lucy was Caleb's wife, and she offered a silent prayer of thanks for that as she took her list to the counter.

six

The wagon, laden with food stuffs, fabric, and planks of wood, lumbered along the road. Bits of mud, left from the melted snow, flew up from the wagon wheels. Caleb risked a glance at Lucy. She hadn't said much, and Caleb had to wonder if she was angry. She didn't look angry, though; she looked tired and sad. Guilt smote him, but he pushed it away. He hadn't asked her to come here. Maybe she had gotten it into her head that he needed her because he couldn't find a wife for himself. Pa had probably led her to believe that.

He hated that Margaret had acted so hurt. There had never been any promises between them, but he had danced with her more than any other woman at the last county dance. And to be honest, his manner had probably indicated his interest. He glanced at the woman beside him. His wife. It still didn't seem real.

She was such a tiny thing, but she was stronger inside than any woman he'd ever met. A tiny Titan. The way she'd shot that mongrel wolf had shocked him to the core. But she still wasn't the wife he wanted. And why was that? Was it because he hadn't picked her for himself? A man wanted to choose his own wife. Not that she wasn't attractive. Maybe that was half the trouble. Being around her made his palms sweaty.

Caleb cleared his throat. "I thought me and Jed would

66

build some more chairs with this lumber. Anything else you can think of, Lucy?"

"Trying to make amends?" she asked softly. "I'm not the one you should apologize to."

So much for extending the olive branch. He scowled. "What do I have to feel guilty about?" Women. Why had Pa gotten him into this predicament?

"What promises did you make that poor woman?"

"I never promised Margaret anything," he said. "I never even asked to call on her."

Lucy tipped her head to the side and looked at him with those clear, honest eyes. After a long moment in which he held her gaze, she nodded. "I see that's true. Poor Margaret."

There was true compassion in her voice, and Caleb had to wonder about this woman who was his wife. He would have felt rivalry toward another man, but Lucy seemed to see right to a person's heart and feel something that mattered. She truly was sorry about Margaret's pain.

Eileen nestled her head under his arm, and Caleb looked down in surprise. The little girl's long lashes lay soft against her pink cheeks, and his heart softened. His life was changing already, and parts of it felt mighty good. He wrapped his arm around Eileen and pulled her close so she didn't jerk so badly when the wagon hit the ruts in the road.

Lucy brushed the blond hair back from Eileen's face. "She's tuckered out. I think we all are."

"I shouldn't have made you come to town so quick."

"It's all right. I had to face them all sooner or later."

"Later would've been better. I should've given you time."

"It wasn't your fault. I'm the interloper, the one who

snatched a handsome, eligible man out from under their noses."

Lucy's voice was matter-of-fact, but Caleb caught his breath. Was that really the way she saw him? A warm glow of pleasure spread through his chest. Women had flirted with him before, but he'd always thought it was simply because he was a Stanton. He didn't want to be loved because of who his pa was, but for who he was.

He hunched his shoulders and stared ahead at the road. Her words were likely a ploy to make sure he didn't send her packing. His lips tightened. How could he do that? If what Pa said was true, he was tied to this woman for life. Divorce wasn't an option, in spite of his blustering when he'd first learned of his pa's actions. He ducked his head deeper into his coat. If there was a way out of this tangle, he didn't see it.

The cabin looked cold and forlorn when they stopped at the barn. This probably wasn't what she expected when Pa told her of all their holdings. And he had never intended to bring a bride to this hovel; it was only a temporary cabin until he built a real house. It might have been good enough for his parents once, but that was in the frontier days. Lucy probably wouldn't have agreed to Pa's ridiculous offer if she'd realized she would be living in a small cabin.

Clouds gathered overhead, and cold drops of rain splashed onto Caleb's face. The wind freshened, and he squinted at the sky. "Storm's coming."

He jumped to the ground and held out his arms for Eileen. Lucy passed her down to him, and he held the little girl close to protect her from as much wetness as he could.

"Jed, help your sister down, then see to the animals," he

said. "When you're done, start bringing in the supplies. I'll be right out to help you."

"Yes, Sir." Jed jumped from the wagon. He helped Lucy down, then led the horses inside the barn.

The rain began to come down in earnest, hard droplets that chilled him instantly. Caleb took Lucy's arm, then they ran toward the house, splashing through the rivulets of mud that were already beginning to fill the yard.

He threw open the door and followed Lucy inside. It wasn't as cold as he had expected; heat still radiated from the last of the fire. The rain drummed on the tin roof as he handed Eileen to Lucy, then went to stir up the embers of the fire.

As he poked at the fire, he heard Lucy humming in a low voice as she rattled pans at the cookstove. It was a homey sound that he found he rather liked. He spent little time here, usually only sleeping on his pallet after a hard day with the cattle. The cabin was changed already after just a few hours.

He pushed the thought away and went out to join Jed in the barn. The lad had already curried the horses and unloaded the wagon. The house supplies were stacked in one corner, and he'd put the feed in the grain bins.

"Good job, Jed," Caleb said.

The boy flushed, and his eyes brightened. "Thank you, Sir."

"You don't have to call me Sir, Boy. Call me Caleb."

"Does that mean you're going to keep us?" Jed's voice was anxious, but he held Caleb's gaze without looking away.

Caleb hesitated. What did he say to that? He really didn't

have a choice. He was coming to realize that after only two days. Pa's health wouldn't take any more upheaval, and the marriage was legal. The best thing was to make do with the situation as best he could. And he had to admit having a pretty wife to come home to might not be such a bad thing.

Jed's face fell as the silence went on. "Don't blame Lucy for us being here, Mr. Stanton. It was my fault." He hung his head. "I stole from your pa as a dare. That's how he met Lucy."

Caleb caught his breath. He would never have guessed Jed would do something like that. He studied the boy's downcast face, then gently touched his shoulder.

"Pa is a pretty good judge of character," he said. "If he thought you weren't a budding Jesse James, I reckon I should give you a second chance as well."

When Jed raised his head, his eyes were glistening with tears. "You won't be sorry, Mr. Stanton. I know Lucy is little, but you don't know her very well yet. Mrs. Thomas at the millinery shop was always going on about how quick she was to learn something new. She'll learn to help you here at the ranch. And I'm a hard worker." He flexed the muscles on his arm. "See here? I can heft a bale of hay by myself. And me and Eileen will try to stay out of your way as much as possible so you can have time with Lucy."

A lump grew in Caleb's throat. Lucy inspired a lot of love in her brother. He squeezed Jed's shoulder. "I'll be glad to have the help, Son. You don't need to stay out of the way. I don't have much experience with young 'uns since I never had a brother, but I'll try to be a dad to you as well. Tomorrow I'll start teaching you how to rope and brand. We'll be taking the cattle to market come summer, and I'll need all the hands I can get."

Jed's lip trembled, and the tears spilled over onto his cheeks. He scrubbed at his face with the back of his hand. "I ain't usually a bawl baby, Mr. Stanton. I'll work hard and make you glad you married us. Lucy's worked so hard to try to keep us together. Now it's my turn."

Us. He reckoned a package deal was what it was, too. He had a ready-made family. It was a little overwhelming.

Caleb cleared his throat. "How about helping me carry this stuff to your sister? She may be a miracle worker, but she has to have something to work with."

"Yes, *Sir*!" Jed hefted a sack of flour to his shoulder and marched toward the house. He looked back at Caleb. "Uh, Mr. Stanton, I'd sure be glad if you didn't say nothing to Lucy about our talk. She hates for people to say nice stuff about her."

"She does?"

Jed nodded vigorously. "There was a guy hanging around all last summer who went on and on about how pretty she was. She finally got fed up and told him the only beauty she was interested in was that on the inside, and since all he could see was the outside, he'd best mosey on down the road."

Caleb squelched a grin. "I'll keep mum."

"Thanks, Mr. Stanton." Jed started for the door.

"Jed."

The boy stopped. "Yes, Sir?"

"Call me Caleb. Mr. Stanton is my pa."

Jed's eyes grew bright. "Yes, Sir, I mean Caleb." He was still grinning as he dashed out into the driving rain.

Caleb grabbed a gunnysack full of food and slung it over

his shoulder. Lucy was quite a remarkable young woman. How many women would have worked so hard and sacrificed so much for their siblings? His respect for his new wife went up a notch.

When he got to the house, Jed was jabbering excitedly while Lucy listened. "I'm going to learn to rope a steer and brand, Lucy. Maybe I'll even get to go on the cattle drive up north. You know how good I can ride."

"We'll see, Jed. That's a big job, and you're not hardly old enough."

"Old enough to do a man's job," Caleb observed, setting his burden on the floor. "Jed's going to be a fine ranch hand."

"He's only twelve, Mr. Stanton."

"I was ten when I went on my first cattle drive."

Lucy's eyes narrowed. "He's my brother, and I'll decide what's best for him!"

Caleb's warm, fuzzy feelings toward Lucy evaporated like the morning dew. She would make a sissy of the boy. "You want Jed to turn into a man or young hoodlum?"

Lucy's face whitened, and she held up her hand as if to ward off a blow. Jed made a small sound of protest, and Caleb realized he'd said too much. "I'm sorry, I didn't mean that. Jed is a fine boy, but he's almost a man, Lucy. You have to let loose those apron strings a tad."

Her sober blue eyes regarded him for a moment, then she nodded. "You may be right. But Jed and Eileen are my whole life. I couldn't bear for anything to happen to Jed."

"You have to trust someone, Lucy. I'm your husband now. I'll take care of Jed."

Her eyes examined him again. "I'm sure you will, Mr.

Stanton," she said softly. "I'm sorry if I made you think I didn't trust you." She turned back to her task of stashing the supplies.

What had Pa been thinking? Did he have any idea how hard it was to be married to a stranger? It would take years to know all about Lucy. Yet Caleb found the thought was not at all unappealing.

❧

Emotions she didn't know she had churned in Lucy's stomach. Anger and jealousy—over her brother, of all things! For so long, she was the one Jed looked up to, the one whose approval he sought. The adoring look Jed gave Caleb had hit her hard. For a moment she felt adrift, a waif in a foster home. Without a needy brother and sister giving her life purpose, what would happen to her? The thought filled her with panic.

Eileen stirred from her pallet on the floor beside Bridget. The little girl sat up and rubbed her eyes. "I'm hungry, Lucy," she said plaintively.

At least Eileen still needed her. "Supper will be ready in about a half an hour," Lucy told her. "Why don't you take Bridget outside until it's ready? The best thing for that hurt leg is some exercise. Otherwise it will stiffen up."

The dog wagged her tail at the mention of her name. She was smart, Lucy observed. She'd figured out they were talking about her.

"Do you need me for anything right now?" Jed asked. His gaze followed Eileen and the dog longingly.

"No, just keep an eye on your sister," Caleb answered before Lucy could.

Outrage churned again. It was *her* job to give or deny

permission. She bit her lip and looked down at the biscuits she was making. *Help me, Lord. My attitude is not worthy of You. I should be glad Caleb is taking an interest in the children. Help me to let go.*

Her heart a bit calmer, she patted the dough, then used her knife to cut the dough into square biscuits. Transferring them to a baking sheet, she slid them into the oven and closed the door. Jed followed Eileen and Bridget outside.

Lucy didn't dare meet Caleb's gaze. She was acting like a shrew, hardly the type of helpmeet she'd wanted to be. She had longed for someone to help her carry the load, so why was she now resenting it when Caleb offered to share some of her burden? Tears blurred her vision.

She heard movement behind her, then Caleb put his hands on her shoulders and turned her to face him. His fingers tilted her chin up, but she stubbornly kept her eyes fastened on his shirt.

"Don't fight me, Lucy. If this marriage is going to make it, we have to work together."

Her heart jumped. He almost sounded as though he *wanted* them to work things out, as if he wasn't planning on shipping her back to Boston the minute his father was well enough to handle the news. She dared a glance into his face. His gray eyes were gentle.

"What are you saying?" she whispered.

He took off his cowboy hat with a swipe of his big hand. "I'm saying that I'm willing to try if you are." He gave a heavy sigh. "We haven't gotten off on a very good start, Lucy, but it seems this marriage is square and legal. We may not love each other, but we can at least be friends and see what happens. I like you, Lucy. You've got guts, even if you are small and spindly."

He grinned, and she smiled back feebly. She wet her lips. "What do you expect of me?" Against her will, she glanced at the ladder leading to the loft.

His cheeks reddened. "Not that," he said hastily. "Not yet, at any rate. You stay with Jed and Eileen. Jed can help in the field while you and Eileen take care of the house."

"I thought you wanted a wife who could rope and shoot as well as a man." She didn't want him to settle for her if she wasn't what he needed in his life.

He grinned. "You sure shoot as well as any man I ever saw." Her cheeks burned, and she ducked her head. He laughed out loud. "I don't think either one of us knows what we want in a mate. We're going to have to discover that as we go along. You willing to try?"

Her throat felt tight, and she struggled not to cry. "I'll try, Mr. Stanton," she managed.

"Like I just told Jed, Mr. Stanton is my pa. Think you can see your way clear to calling me Caleb? Seeing as we're married and all."

Her gaze searched his, and she nodded. "I'll try, Caleb."

"I will, too." His gaze was soft and roamed down to her lips. His grin widened, then his eyes grew sober. "Can I kiss you, Lucy?"

Her heart fluttered like a frightened bird. She'd never been kissed, and she wanted to wait until she felt more than mere liking for a man. But this was her husband; how did she refuse him such a natural request? Before she could answer, his fingers tightened on her shoulders, and he bent his head. His lips grazed her cheek.

Her stomach felt funny, all nervous and fluttery. Then he pulled away.

"That's all for now," he said. "When you're ready for a real kiss, you let me know." He sauntered to the door with a smug grin as if he knew her knees were almost too weak to hold her.

When the door closed behind him, Lucy sank into a chair. If a kiss on the cheek affected her like this, what would a real kiss do? She was almost afraid to find out. She'd had no experience with men to gauge her reaction; maybe this was how a woman always felt. But she didn't think she'd feel like this if her old landlord, Amos Cramer, kissed her on the cheek.

seven

Caleb heard every sound in the room below him all night long. Jed groaned several times in his sleep; Lucy was up taking Eileen to the outhouse several times, and he thought he heard soft weeping at one point near dawn. He thought about climbing down from the loft to see who it was, but he knew he didn't have the right words to fix the problem if it was Lucy.

He rolled over and punched his straw pillow into shape. It was prickly and uncomfortable; he was used to the feather pillow, now propping Lucy's head. How did he get into this situation? Pa must be going senile to have come up with this plan. He and Lucy were worlds apart in their temperaments and goals. He tended to think things through, to plod along with careful plans. Lucy seemed to rush in with no thought for consequences. Look at the way she'd demanded he get rid of his pet tarantula, just an instant decision with no forethought.

Marriage should be a partnership like a business. He would have been better off with someone who knew ranching and intended to help him reach his goals, someone who wasn't so flighty and emotional. Emotion made him antsy. He grimaced, remembering the fear he'd seen in her face. When he'd asked to kiss her last night, she'd obviously thought he intended to claim his husbandly rights. Her blue eyes had been huge, and she looked as though she wanted to bolt for the door.

She was a pretty little thing. He'd have to be a eunuch not to think about what it would be like to be truly married to her in every sense of the word, but he wasn't an ogre. Caleb didn't like being thought of that way, either. Still, he had to admit he'd liked the reaction his impersonal kiss had brought. Those soft cheeks had bloomed color like the first rosy blush of dawn. Maybe they had physical attraction going for them, but that was all. In every other way, they were just too different. And he didn't know what to do about it.

He'd either have to change or she would. And he had the feeling they were both a little too set in their ways to do much changing. Cheeper, the rooster, crowed from the chicken coop out back, and Caleb sighed. Those cattle weren't getting herded into the south pasture by themselves. In spite of having little or no sleep, he had to get up.

As he swung his feet to the floor, he heard the rattle of pans in the room below. He raised an eyebrow. Who was up so early and why? He pulled on his boots and climbed down the ladder. Jed yawned at the kitchen table while Lucy, her glorious blond hair still hanging down her back, poked life into the cookstove fire. She was already dressed in a blue gingham dress.

Jed saw him first. "Morning, Mr. Stanton."

"Call me Caleb, remember?" he said, his eyes on the way the lamplight lit Lucy's hair with shimmering lights.

"Yes, Sir."

Lucy turned and caught his stare. A becoming bloom of color raced up her cheeks, but she bravely met his gaze. He saw the muscles in her neck move as she swallowed, then she turned around quickly and took some eggs out of a bowl.

"Jed got me some eggs this morning. I hope that's all right," she said without looking at him.

"Of course. I wasn't expecting you to get out of bed so early. You had a busy day yesterday."

"So did you. I heard you tossing and turning all night."

"You didn't seem to get much sleep, either," he pointed out.

Bridget nosed his leg, and Caleb looked down. "You want out, Girl?"

The dog whined, and he went to the door and pushed it open. Bridget gave a deep bark and sprang out the door. Barking furiously, she raced to the road and planted her feet wide as she growled and barked at a dim figure by the gate.

Caleb squinted through the dim light of predawn. A rider on a horse. Not willing to take any chances, he shut the door and stepped to the back door, where his rifle leaned against the wall. He checked to make sure it was loaded, then swung open the front door.

Drew Larson pushed past him. "Put the peashooter away. We need to talk."

Scowling, Caleb tightened his grip on his rifle. "I've got nothing to say to you, Larson. You've stolen the last of my cattle. The next time I'll shoot first and ask questions later."

Drew wasn't listening. His mouth hung open as he stared at Lucy. Then a slow smile lit his swarthy face. "Hello, Honey, where did you come from?" He started toward Lucy.

Caleb stepped in front of him. "You're not welcome

here, Larson. And that's my wife you're ogling." It took all his effort not to plant his fist in the man's face.

Drew's chin dropped further. "Your wife? I didn't hear nothing about no wedding. When I worked here just five days ago you didn't say nothing about getting hitched. What are you trying to pull, Stanton? Her kind is fair game."

Caleb clenched his teeth, his throat tight. He grabbed Drew by the collar and propelled him back toward the door. "She's a lady, Larson, and my wife. Now get your slimy presence out of our house and don't come back."

"I'm working for the Burnett ranch now, and I got a proposition for you."

"I'm not interested in anything you have to say. Does Burk know you're a cattle thief? I'd venture he would be interested in that piece of information."

Drew's mouth curled in a snarl. "You keep your trap shut if you know what's good for you, Stanton! You spill any of your lies, and I'll tell him about that bull of his you let stay with the herd last summer."

Caleb's brows drew together. "I'd ask what you were talking about, but I'm in no mood to hear more of your lies. You know as well as I do that I've never taken so much as a blade of grass that didn't belong to me. Now get your lazy carcass out of my sight. If I see you on Stanton land again, I'll shoot."

Drew gave a derisive laugh. "You don't have the guts, Stanton. Now your pa, that would be a different story, but I got nothing to fear from you. Your religion has made you too soft." He touched his hat, his gaze again on Lucy. "Morning, Miss. I'm sure we'll run into each other again."

Lucy was backed up against the stove, her eyes wide and

her lips white. She didn't answer Drew, and he gave a short laugh and spun on his heel. He slammed the door behind him.

Caleb let out the breath he didn't even realize he was holding. His jaw hurt from clenching it, and his heart was stuttering like a faulty steam engine. "I'm sorry, Lucy," he said. "He won't bother you again."

Lucy gulped. "Can he get you in trouble, Caleb?"

Caleb laughed, a mirthless sound. "He can spread his lies, but Burk isn't one to go off half-cocked. He'd come to me for an answer. And by the time he hears any of Drew Larson's lies, he will have found out what kind of man he has working for him and fired him, most likely. Larson is—well, I won't say what I really think. You just see you avoid him if he happens to be in town the same time as you." His scowl deepened as he thought of the way the man had talked about Lucy. No one talked about his wife like that!

His wife. When he was least expecting it, that fact reared up and hit him in the face again. He stared at Lucy. No wonder Larson was bowled over. She looked delectable. No one who looked that good could be a wife. Small, but exquisitely proportioned, she looked like a china doll come to life with her golden ringlets and perfect skin. He stared into her eyes and wondered what she would do if he took a step nearer.

He mentally shook himself. He had work to do; there was no time to be inside mooning over a woman. This was going to have to be a working relationship, and he was glad to see Lucy was determined to hold up her end of the bargain.

"I could use some of those flapjacks I smell cooking," he said.

Lucy blinked as though she had forgotten what she was doing, then blushed and turned back to the stove. "The gravy is done, and the eggs will be in a minute. Jed fetched some clean water for you to wash up in."

He stared at his hands. "I don't need the water."

Lucy whirled and pointed a spatula at him. "Caleb Stanton, this may be Texas, but where I come from, we wash up for meals. I won't have dirty hands at my table."

"My hands are clean. See." He held them out for her inspection.

She didn't look at his hands but stared him in the eye and pointed to the bowl and pitcher. "The soap is there as well."

"If you think we're running a cattle ranch like a millinery shop, you'll soon find out different. I don't have time to fuss with soap and water every time I want to eat. You can get that through your head right now!"

Her eyes welled with tears, but she put her hands on her hips and faced him down. "And your father wants some genteel manners brought to this spread. You'll wash your hands, or you'll go without breakfast."

He weakened at the sight of her tears. Caleb gritted his teeth, then stalked to the bowl of water. Snatching up the cake of soap, he lathered his hands, then poured water over them. "Satisfied?" He held them up. "Next time you want to 'genteel' someone, try Pa. He's the one who signed on for this nonsense, not me."

"Thank you, Caleb. Please sit down and eat your breakfast while it's hot." Lucy's voice was composed, but he could still see a suspicious wetness in her eyes.

"That's what I wanted to do an hour ago," he muttered.

He caught a glimmer of a grin on Jed's face. "What are you grinning about?" he demanded.

"Nothing," the boy said hastily, stuffing a flapjack into his mouth.

"Jed, what have I told you about talking with your mouth full?" his sister said. "And I didn't hear either of you pray."

Caleb exchanged a commiserating smile with Jed. At least he wasn't the only one in hot water, he reflected as he bowed his head.

❧

Lucy kept a small plate of flapjacks hot on top of the cookstove. Eileen would be hungry when she awakened. Tomorrow, she would make sure they all ate together. Eileen had been awake most of the night, though, and she would be cranky without her rest. Lucy felt a little cranky herself. Maybe she had come off too domineering over the washing up, but she wasn't about to start off this marriage by letting a man eat at her table without washing his hands. She'd worked for years to get Jed in the habit, and Caleb could destroy all her hard work in the blink of an eye.

She had her work cut out for her. Caleb was used to being around only men; he had no concept of the niceties of life. But she would set such a good spread for him; he would be willing to do whatever he had to do to eat her cooking. She'd learned to cook at Mama's knee, and she was good at it.

Lucy heated water on the stove to wash the dishes, then got out the ingredients to make bread. Kneading it with practiced hands, she put it on to raise, then went through the cabin and collected all the dirty clothes. She'd noticed a pile of Caleb's clothes in the pantry, of all places.

By the time Eileen had gotten up, Lucy had hauled in wood and water to do laundry. She fed her sister, then set her to helping hang the clothes up to dry on some string Lucy strung up by the fire.

Humming as she worked, she baked a raisin pie, then rolled out noodles and left them on the table to dry. What a blessing it was to have chickens and eggs in the backyard. God had truly blessed her. As she'd tossed in the night, she had come to that conclusion. Caleb was a fine man, a bit rough around the edges, but he just wasn't used to women. She would be patient and be the helpmeet she was created to be. Caleb would be glad for his father's meddling in the end.

Dinner was ready by one. In fact, if the men didn't come in soon, the noodles would be overcooked, and the chicken would be dry as chalk. Lucy kept glancing worriedly through the window, but saw no sign of her menfolk. By one-thirty she was becoming angry, and by two, she was downright livid. It was the height of inconsideration to let this fine food go to waste. She couldn't help but wonder if Caleb had done it deliberately to get her back for making him wash his hands.

"We might as well eat without them, Eileen," she said. Lifting her sister onto the chair, she ladled up rubbery noodles and stringy chicken. It tasted as bad as it looked. Eileen picked at her plate, and Lucy finally gave her a piece of warm bread spread with butter and jam. By the time she put Eileen down for her nap, Lucy's anger was white-hot.

She rehearsed all the things she would say to Caleb when he got in. And Jed. He knew better.

She started to dump the remains of the meal into a dish to give to Bridget when she got back with the men, then stopped and stared at the food. They would just have to eat it. Where she came from, food was a precious commodity; it didn't deserve to be dumped out. If it was not the best now, maybe that would teach Mr. Caleb Stanton to be on time for a meal next time.

Lucy put the pan back on the stove to stay warm, then felt the clothes hanging around the cabin. They were dry, so she took them down and folded them. She carried Caleb's up the ladder to his room. His bed had not been made, and she clicked her tongue at her forgetfulness. She would have to remember tomorrow.

She threw the covers up over the bed, and her foot hit something under the bed. Curious, she knelt and peered in the darkness. A battered metal box, about six inches by eight inches was the only thing under the bed. She laid a hand on the cool surface and pulled it to her. For a moment she hesitated. Maybe it was something private. But she was his wife, and they should have no secrets from one another, she told herself.

Slowly, she opened the lid. Inside was a journal and a daguerreotype. Lucy picked up the photo. It was of a young woman holding a baby. She had a look about her that reminded her of Caleb, and Lucy realized she was looking at Caleb's mother. She was lovely, with a cloud of thick, dark hair and Caleb's stubborn mouth and expressive eyes.

A lump in her throat, Lucy dropped the picture back into the box and picked up the journal. It looked old, too old to be Caleb's personal journal. The battered leather cover felt loved and worn in her hand, and the pages smelled old and stale.

She opened the first page. Mary Elizabeth Stanton. His mother's journal. Tears stung Lucy's eyes. Poor motherless boy. This was all he had of his mother, all the experience he had of women as well, just some brief memories of a long-dead mother. No wonder his father was determined to find him a wife.

Lucy put the journal back into the box. She couldn't read it, not without Caleb's permission and knowledge. It was too private, almost sacred. Her anger mostly evaporated, she finished making the bed, then dropped the freshly folded clothes into a box that served as Caleb's chest.

She had just finished putting the clothes away when she heard a horse neigh in the yard. Compressing her lips, she glanced out the window. Jed was still mounted, but Caleb had jumped to the ground and was opening the barn door. Lucy lifted the watch that hung around her neck. The watch had belonged to her mama and offered her some comfort as she checked the time. Four o'clock, almost time for supper, and the uneaten dinner sat congealing on the stove. Her anger raged again, and she went down to meet them.

eight

Caleb was bone-weary, and his stomach was gnawing on his backbone. Jed had made several pointed comments about dinner around about one o'clock, but he'd ignored him. The lad needed to grow up and realize that a man didn't go running home when his belly got a little empty. He didn't go home until the work was done.

"Help me curry the horses, and we'll see if Lucy can rustle us up some grub," he told Jed.

The boy's shoulders drooped wearily, and Caleb almost relented, then remembered he was supposed to be teaching Jed how to be a man. He was responsible for Jed now. He shoved open the sliding door to the barn and led his horse inside. He grabbed a curry brush, then handed one to Jed. They quickly curried the horses and turned them out into the stable. Caleb tossed a pitchfork full of hay over the fence, then clapped Jed on the back.

"You did a man's work today, Jed. I was mighty proud of you."

Jed's chest visibly swelled, and if his grin were any bigger, it would have split his face. "Thank you, Sir."

"You as hungry as I am?"

Jed nodded. "Lucy is probably wondering where we are."

"We're early, why should she wonder?"

"We usually eat at one at home."

"She knew we were working." Caleb started toward the house.

A strange aroma wafted toward him when he pushed open the door. It smelled a bit like something charred and a bit like glue. Whatever it was, it didn't smell good. Jed had been bragging on his sister's cooking, but it must have been the youngster's love talking. Still, Caleb would put a good face on it and force it down. He was hungry enough to eat whatever she threw at him.

He forced a smile. "Smells like something's cooking."

Lucy stood and put her fists on her hips. "Something *was* cooking. Now something is burned. But help yourself." She made a sweeping gesture toward the cookstove. "If you dare." Her eyebrows lifted in challenge.

Caleb looked at Jed, and Jed looked at Caleb. Caleb knew he wore the same expression the boy did. A look of panic and dismay. He sidled over to the stove and looked in the pan. It might have been chicken and noodles once, but now it more resembled a sticky gob of glue.

"Uh, looks good," he said lamely. Lucy almost visibly swelled, and he was reminded of an outraged mother hen.

"It *was* good around one o'clock. Even at two it was still edible. Now it looks—it looks like porridge!" Lucy stalked toward the fireplace and sat beside Eileen. Even her back and neck looked outraged.

Caleb scratched his head and looked at Jed. The boy's eyes were round and pleading, and he stared from the mess on the stove to Caleb.

"Do we have to eat it?" he whispered.

"I heard that, and the answer is yes!" Lucy jumped to her feet again. "Maybe it will help you remember to come home in time to eat tomorrow."

Caleb frowned. This was not going the way he had pictured the evening. He'd planned to eat a hot, home-cooked meal, then take the buggy over to the main house and check on Pa.

"I see I need to explain the way a ranch works," he began.

"No, I need to explain the way a cook works," Lucy said, springing to her feet. "When food is ready to be eaten, the men come and eat it. Jed is a growing boy. He needs to eat three square meals a day. Look at him, Caleb. He's skinny as a pitchfork and needs fattening. That's one reason I agreed to marry you. And you need to eat three square meals a day. If you can't be bothered to come home for dinner, then you need to tell me, and I'll pack you a lunch or bring it to you."

He looked at Jed. She was right. His heart clenched at the boy's thinness. He bit his lip and looked back at Lucy. Her cheeks were rosy with anger, and her blue eyes sparkled. Her beauty tugged at him. If the children weren't there, he would have pulled her into his arms and kissed her.

His anger subsided and he grinned. "A bit riled, aren't you? You sure look pretty that way. Maybe we'll have to try this again tomorrow, Jed."

Her brother grinned, though his eyes were still anxious. He'd obviously been made to toe the line by his sister before.

For a moment, the color in Lucy's cheeks deepened. Then the corner of her mouth lifted, and she bit her lip. Her dimple appeared, and she clapped a hand over her mouth. A chuckle squeaked past her lips.

"Don't think fake compliments will make me forgive you," she said. Though her tone was severe, her eyes held a hint of mirth.

He held up his hands. "Uncle!" He turned to Jed. "She has me, Boy. I should have realized you would need to be fed. But we'll take our punishment like men, what do you say?"

Jed gave a doubtful glare at the mess in the pan. "Do we have to?"

"Are you a man or a rabbit? Come on, this will taste better than it looks." He grabbed the ladle and tried to scoop some out of the pan. It stuck to the spoon and refused to drop to the plate.

"I think I'll be a rabbit today," Jed said.

Lucy sighed and got to her feet. "Since you're truly contrite, I'll see if I can find something edible for you."

Caleb shook the spoon again. The glob clung steadfastly to the spoon. He dropped it back into the pan with a sigh of relief. "Jed and I will rise up and call you blessed, won't we, Boy?"

"I'll even tell everyone she's the prettiest woman in Boston, if I don't have to eat that slop," Jed said.

"Boston, my foot! She's the prettiest woman in the Red River Valley—in Texas even," Caleb said. He caught Lucy by the waist as she sashayed past him. She smelled good, kind of like fresh-baked bread. "Do you forgive us?"

"I forgive Jed. I haven't decided about you yet," she said. Her lashes lowered to her cheeks, then she raised them, and he was dazzled by the light in her eyes.

For the second time, he wished the kids weren't here. How was he supposed to woo his wife with a constant audience? It would be a challenge, but for the first time Caleb realized he intended to do just that. Almost against his will, his hands tightened around her waist, and he pulled her against his chest and rested his chin on her head.

"You're staying right here until you tell me I'm forgiven," he said softly.

She struggled to get free for a moment, but then her arms circled his waist, and she stood content in his arms. "I'm not complaining," she said too softly for the kids to hear.

His heart soared. She must find him attractive. Maybe even as attractive as he found her. The Bible admonished him to love his wife. He was beginning to realize that might not be too difficult.

2º

The days sped by in a blur of busyness. Lucy had so much to learn she felt her head must surely explode with the knowledge she stuffed in. She and Caleb were still wary around one another, but they were slowly learning to know one another.

Spring had finally come to Texas. Wildflowers brought welcome bits of color to the landscape, and the air was filled with the fragrance of spring. Lucy carted her washtub outside and scrubbed the clothes while Eileen occupied herself planting her own small garden.

Lucy rubbed at a spot on Caleb's dungarees. Her hands were red and chapped, but who would have thought she would find such satisfaction in caring for a man and his belongings? Caleb's prediction about the softness of her hands had proven true, but Lucy didn't mind. Her red hands were proof of the effort she was putting into this marriage.

She hung the clothes on the line Caleb had put up for her

and went to the house to start dinner. Caleb had told her he would be in the south pasture all day and had asked her to bring the meal to him. Since that one missed meal, he had been conscientious about keeping her informed of his mealtime activities. She suppressed a grin.

"Eileen, it's time to come in," she called.

She went inside and took the bread from the breadbox. Cutting thick slices, she made egg sandwiches, then wrapped them in cloth and put them in a box. To that she added cheese and pie she'd made earlier in the day.

She cocked her head and listened. Eileen still hadn't answered her. She went to the back door. "Eileen, come in now!" There was still no answer, so she stepped outside. She sighed when she saw no sign of her sister. Eileen was probably in the barn petting the calf.

Lucy hurried across the yard to the barn. They would have to hurry, or Caleb would accuse her of ignoring his mealtime. She shoved open the barn door and stepped into the dimly lit barn. A shaft of sunlight illuminated the dust motes, and the straw made her sneeze.

"Eileen?"

The only answer she got was the snort of the horse in the far stall and the rustle as the calf shuffled in the hay. Beginning to be alarmed, Lucy turned and ran back to the front yard. "Eileen! Where are you?" She raced around the house several times before she could admit the obvious to herself. Eileen was nowhere to be found.

Her heart was racing like a runaway train, and her mouth was dry with panic. Shading her eyes, she stared out at the horizon. Where could Eileen be? Lucy was torn between wandering out to find Eileen herself or going for help. Her heart screamed for her to find her sister now, but wisdom dictated finding Caleb. He knew the area; she didn't.

She threw the sidesaddle on Wanda and clambered atop the mare's broad back. Digging her heels into Wanda's sides, she clung desperately to the pommel as the horse broke into a canter. Within minutes, she was in sight of the herd of longhorn and could make out Caleb's familiar broad shoulders.

At the sight of her husband, tears sprang from her eyes, and she began to sob. "Caleb!" she screamed. The sound that came out of her mouth was closer to a croak.

Caleb's head came up, and he kicked his horse into a run, with Jed right behind him. "What is it? What's wrong?" His gaze darted past her. "Where's Eileen?"

"She's gone! I was doing laundry, and she was playing with Bridget. When I called her for lunch, she was missing." Aware she was beginning to babble, Lucy took a deep breath. "I didn't know where to look."

Caleb turned and whistled. "Bridget, come here, Girl!" The dog came bounding to him.

Hope lifted its head for a brief instant. "Do you think Bridget can find her?"

"She loves Eileen. She'll find her."

They turned and rode back to the cabin.

"I'll look around just to make sure," Caleb said. "Did you check the privy?"

"No, I didn't think of that." Lucy rushed to the privy and threw open the door. Empty. Her shoulders drooping, she followed Caleb as he quickly walked around the yard and then checked the barn.

He knelt and took Bridget's head in his hands. "Find

Eileen, Bridget." He released her. "Go, find Eileen!"

Bridget barked and began sniffing the ground. She circled the privy, then went around to the front. She paused at Eileen's small garden plot and then tore off toward the north.

"Quick, get the horses, we'll follow her!"

Lucy wanted to just run after her, but she realized she'd never keep up with the dog. She grabbed Wanda's reins and managed to mount by herself. Caleb and Jed were already ahead of her. She bounced hard in the saddle as Wanda strove to catch them.

She could hear Bridget barking as she made her way toward a meadow by the river. The river! Eileen loved water. Her heart in her mouth, Lucy bent low over Wanda's neck and smacked her hand on the horse's rump.

"Eileen!" she shouted.

Caleb and Jed reached the grove of trees, and Lucy got there a moment later. Panting nearly as hard as Wanda, she looked around for her sister. Nothing.

"We'll check the river. You look around," Caleb said. His voice was grim, and Lucy's eyes filled with tears as she watched him and Jed stalk purposefully toward the river. She could hear the rushing water from here. The Red River could be deadly this time of year.

Then she heard Bridget give a joyful bark. The dog was leaping happily into the air. Lucy looked closer and saw the still form of her sister on the ground. She rushed to Eileen and reached her just as the little girl sat up and rubbed her eyes sleepily. Bridget licked her face, and Eileen began to cry.

Lucy scooped her into her arms and hugged her fiercely.

"Here she is," she shouted.

"Lucy, you're hurting me," Eileen complained.

Lucy wanted to loosen her grip, but she couldn't let go. "I thought I'd lost you," she whispered. "Don't ever do that again, Eileen. You know better than to go off without telling me."

Jed and Caleb came running. Jed's face was streaked from tears, and Caleb's eyes were bright with relief. Jed took his sister from Lucy, and she wrapped her arms and legs around him.

"I looked for you, Jed, but you was hiding," she said reproachfully. "I walked and walked, but you weren't there."

Caleb held out his arms for Eileen, and she went to him. He set her on the ground and knelt beside her. "Eileen, what did I tell you about watching out for Lucy?"

She hung her head. "You said to stay close to her all the time, so's I could see her."

"That's right. What did you do today?"

Eileen started to cry. "I just wanted to find you and Jed. I wanted Jed to see my flowers."

"I know, Sweetheart, but you disobeyed me. You know what that means, don't you?" Caleb's voice was gentle but firm.

"I have to be punished?" Eileen said hesitantly. Her tears flowed in earnest now.

Caleb nodded. "I'm afraid so."

"Caleb, no!" Lucy said. "I'm just glad to have her back safe and sound."

He took Lucy's hand and led her away from the children. "Eileen knew the rules, Lucy. If we let her get away with it this time, she might not remember how important this rule is the next time. The next time she could drown or Indians could find her first. I'm responsible for her now, and this is the way it has to be."

Lucy's eyes burned from all the tears she'd shed. "I can't stand to hurt her, Caleb. You'll have to do it."

"If that's what you want." He turned and went back to Eileen. He picked her up and went to his horse. "We'll discuss what the punishment is to be when we get home."

Lucy's mouth was dry with dread as she mounted her horse and followed Jed and Caleb home. She knew Caleb was right, but that didn't make it easier. It had always been hard for her to discipline Eileen, who was so small and engaging. But this had been willful disobedience. She knew she wasn't to leave the yard.

They reached the cabin, and Jed took the horses to the barn. Caleb carried Eileen inside while Lucy followed, her footsteps dragging. He sat on a chair and pulled Eileen onto his lap, then motioned for Lucy to be seated next to him.

"What do you have to say, Eileen?"

"I'm sorry," she wept. "I shouldn't have gone out of the yard. I knew I wasn't s'posed to. I'se sorry, Lucy."

"Lucy was very sad when she found you gone. And we didn't make the rule to be mean. You remember when the mongrel wolf came?"

Eileen nodded. "Lucy shooted it with the gun."

Caleb nodded. "Another wolf could come when Lucy wasn't there with the gun. There are Indians and snakes, too. All kinds of things that could hurt you. We make a rule because we love you. And Jesus is sad when we disobey. Do you want to tell Him you're sorry, too?"

Eileen nodded and clasped her little hands together. "Jesus, I'm sorry," she sobbed. "I didn't want to make You sad, and I didn't want to worry Lucy. Help me be a good girl next time. Amen." She sniveled and wiped her nose with the back of her hand.

Tears burned Lucy's eyes. Wasn't that good enough?

"Am I going to be punished now?" Eileen's voice was pitiful.

"Do you think you should be?" Caleb stroked her hair.

Eileen hesitated before she nodded. "You have to 'cause you said. I wouldn't want God to think you was a liar."

Lucy thought she saw a hint of moisture in Caleb's eyes. He put Eileen down and rose. Stepping across the floor, he took a wooden spoon from the utensil crock.

"I don't want to discipline you, Eileen. Just like God doesn't like to discipline us. Bend over the chair."

Tears streaming down her face, Eileen rose slowly and bent over the chair. Caleb bit his lip and looked at Lucy helplessly. She could see the toll this was taking on him.

He knelt beside Eileen and whacked her three times across the bottom. The licks weren't hard, but Lucy winced each time.

After it was over, Caleb pulled Eileen into his arms. "I love you, Sweetheart. Let's pray and promise God we'll try to obey next time."

Eileen wound her arms around his neck and kissed him. "I love you, Caleb. I'se glad you married us."

"So am I," Caleb said, his gaze meeting Lucy's.

nine

Lucy touched the cow with one hand gingerly and wrinkled her nose at the unlovely aroma of cow and manure. Positioning the bucket under the cow, she grabbed the cow's udder and squeezed. Nothing. She huffed and got a firmer grip. This couldn't be that hard. She'd already watched Caleb do it for two months. If he could do it, she could. Maybe if she sang to the animal. . . .

She cleared her voice and thought of the words to that song Caleb sang. She raised her voice in melody.

"From this valley they say you are going. We will miss your bright eyes and sweet smile. For they say you are taking the sunshine, that brightens our pathway awhile."

She felt stupid singing a love song to a cow. But Bessie seemed to like it. The cow snorted, then swished her tail, and a drop of milk squirted the next time Lucy squeezed. Heartened, she leaned her head against the cow and tried to get a rhythm going. *Squirt, squirt. Ping, ping.* She smiled. She was getting it!

Then Caleb's deep baritone chimed in with her soprano.

"Come and sit by my side if you love me. Do not hasten to bid me adieu. But remember the Red River Valley and the one who has loved you so true."

His gray eyes were smiling as he pulled up a stool beside hers. Did he love her? She was beginning to think he felt something, even as this feeling grew in her own heart. Was

98

it love? She hoped so. She wanted to love her husband. But she'd had so little experience with men. Maybe it was merely physical attraction. Whatever it was, she wanted to nurture it.

"I reckon you're getting the hang of this," Caleb said. "Almost half a bucket."

"You usually get over a bucket."

"I didn't at the beginning. Once those fingers get stronger, you'll be great at it."

Her fingers *did* ache. She flexed them. "You want to finish? Bessie might appreciate being totally emptied." She scooted over to make room for him. His broad shoulder grazed hers, and she could smell the clean scent of the soap he'd used to wash. She wanted to lean against him and have him gather her in his arms the way he'd done that night he'd been too late for dinner. So far there'd been no repeat of that.

Though it was only late April, the weather had turned hot. She could hear Jed shouting to Eileen as he tossed a ball with her in the yard. Bridget ran barking from one to the other. She and Caleb were alone, a state that came so seldom she felt tongue-tied.

"I thought we'd go check on Pa after supper," Caleb said. "We haven't been over for two days. That okay with you?"

"Of course. I made some pies today. I'll take one to him."

"He'll enjoy that. All he's done lately is eat, Percy says. I think Percy is getting tired of cooking for him."

"I wonder if we should take dinner to him for a few days to give Percy a break? I could go over in the morning to cook." She almost hated the thought of leaving her little cabin. It had quickly become home.

"We can ask him." Caleb rose and took the bucket of frothy milk. Lucy followed him, and they crossed the yard to the house. She'd opened the windows to take advantage of what wind there was, and the new yellow gingham curtains blew in the breeze.

"You've done wonders with the house," Caleb said. "I never realized before how much this place needed something. Pa hasn't even seen it yet."

"He'll just say, 'I told you so.'" Lucy smiled and took Caleb's hand.

He gave her a surprised glance, then laced his fingers through hers. A warm glow spread through Lucy's stomach. She prayed every day for the relationship between them to blossom and flourish. It looked as though God was answering that prayer.

The next day Caleb showed Lucy how to hitch the horse to the buggy. "Are you sure you know how to get to the main house?"

"I've been there many times, Caleb," she said with a toss of her head. "I may be small, but I'm not a child." She was an adult and his wife. Sometimes he could be so sweet, and then the next day he would treat her like she was Eileen's age. Lucy tightened the strings on her bonnet and squared her shoulders.

"Sorry." Caleb grinned and put an arm around her.

The hug he gave her felt like one he'd give Eileen, and it irritated her. After the closeness of last night, she wanted him to cradle her in his arms and kiss her, really kiss her. Not that light peck on the cheek he'd taken to giving her every night. How did a woman go about letting a man know she was ready for more than he was offering? Would he think she was wanton? Lucy gave a tiny sigh.

"What's wrong?"

"Nothing." She pulled away and climbed into the buggy without his assistance. She stared into his perplexed gaze and stretched out her arms. "Could you hand Eileen up to me?"

He ran a hand through his hair and sighed. Scooping up Eileen, he handed her to Lucy. "You girls be careful. Don't forget there's a rifle under the seat if you need it."

"I remember." She stared straight ahead and slapped the reins against the mare's back. "Dinner will be at one. Try not to be late."

Caleb reached up and grabbed the reins. "Lucy, what's wrong? Did I do something?"

Shame twisted in her gut. It wasn't his fault she was feeling so blue and rejected. He was doing everything he could to make this work. How was he to know she was ready for a deeper relationship? She bit her lip and raised her gaze to his. "We'll talk tonight, after the kids are in bed."

Relief lit his eyes, and he nodded, though a perplexed frown still marred his forehead. He slapped the mare's hindquarters, and she set off at a trot. As she guided the horse, Lucy stewed about what to say to him. Their relationship seemed to be stagnating. She didn't want a big brother; she wanted a husband. Caleb was trying so hard, too. Half the time she didn't know what she wanted, so how was he supposed to know?

The recent rains had left the ground muddy. Lucy tried to keep the buggy in the driest areas, but she still got bogged down several times. Eileen fell asleep, and Lucy breathed a sigh of relief. Now she could concentrate on where she was going and on her own thoughts. She rounded a curve and hit a deep patch of mud. The mare whinnied and thrashed in the mud, flinging up bits of muck onto Lucy's dress with her hooves.

"Whoa, Girl!" Lucy pulled on the reins and clambered down. The mud sucked at her boots, and she almost fell as she made her way to the horse's head. She patted her and tried to back the horse out of the mud. The horse reared in terror, and Lucy scrambled back. She lost her balance and sat awkwardly in the mud. Struggling to get up, she fell forward. Near tears, she tried to get on all fours, but the mud sucked at her.

She might have to send Eileen for help. She could see the smoke from the main house from here. Then she heard a horse whinny behind her. She turned and looked up into the smiling, swarthy face of Drew Larson.

He tipped his hat. "Morning, Miss."

"That's Missus," she corrected.

His grin widened. "Whatever you say, Ma'am. You need some help? Looks like you're in a bit of a predicament."

His smirk raised Lucy's ire, but she was in no position to refuse help. "I would appreciate it," she said coldly.

"Say that like you mean it, and I might see my way clear to helping you." He put his hands on his hips, and his white teeth flashed.

"Mr. Larson, give me your hand!" She wasn't about to play games with him.

His eyes widened, and he stepped forward and offered his hand. She gripped it with her mud-covered one, and he hauled her inelegantly to her feet. Before she could thank him and release his hand, he gave a tug and jerked her into his arms.

"Now I'll take my appreciation," he said. He bent his head.

Lucy didn't take time to think, she just walloped him upside the head with a glob of mud she'd inadvertently clutched in her other hand. It hit him in the eye, and he let out a yelp. He was so startled, he let loose of her, and she sprang to the buggy and wrested the rifle from under the seat.

"I won't hesitate to use this on a coyote like you, Mr. Larson. I appreciate your help, but not enough to offer more than a handshake and a thank you. Now mosey on down the road. My father-in-law is expecting me, and his men would be rather put out to find you'd manhandled me."

Drew's face suffused with red, and he narrowed his eyes. "We'll meet again, Miss."

"That's *Missus*!" she shouted after him as he vaulted to his horse and wheeled angrily away.

Lucy snapped the whip over the mare's head. "Giddup!" She flipped her filthy skirt around her legs and hunched forward. She couldn't wait to get out of this mud-encased dress. The horse and buggy cantered into the yard. Lucy pulled hard on the reins to halt the horses, then she flung herself from the buggy and scooped up Eileen. Several ranch hands gaped as she hurried to the house. She was wet and scared, but she was determined not to let that bully cow her.

Luther, his spectacles perched on his nose, looked up from where he sat by the window with a book in his hand. His bushy eyebrows rose when he saw her condition, and he stood. "Lucy, what's happened to you?"

"My buggy got bogged down in the mud," she said. He didn't need to worry about Drew; she would take care of her own battles.

"My dear girl, you must get out of those wet clothes." He stood and went to the hall. "Percy, fetch the trunk with Mrs. Stanton's things in it." He turned back to Lucy. "I kept some of my wife's nicer things, since they were all I had of her. You're about the same size. I think they'll fit."

"Oh, I couldn't wear them," Lucy said. "An old pair of dungarees and a shirt will do until I get home."

"Absolutely not!" He gestured for her to sit. "Percy will bring the trunk, and you can take whatever you like."

"Your cushion will be soiled if I sit down. I'll just stand here," she said. She hated to feel like she was asking for anything.

"Here, then." He pulled a ladder-back chair out from the desk.

Gingerly, she eased onto the chair. Flecks of mud fell to the carpet, and she grimaced and sprang to her feet. "I'll get it." She crouched and began to pick up the bits of debris.

"Lucy, please." At the pained look on his face, she stood. "You're not a servant here; you're my daughter. I don't want you acting like you're here on suffrage."

Tears welled in Lucy's eyes. She'd always been so used to carrying her own weight, of trying not to be a bother, that it came hard to accept what he was offering. "Thank you, Mr. Stanton."

Luther smiled. "Do you think you could ever see your way to calling me Pa, like Caleb does? Or even Father would do. I've asked before, but you seem to forget each time that I'm not an ogre."

Lucy's throat closed. "I'd like that—Pa."

Luther colored with pleasure. He knelt beside Eileen's chair. "I'd like you to call me Grandpa, if you'd like, Eileen."

The little girl stared into the older man's face. She put a small hand on each side of his face. "I like you," she announced. "You can be my grandpa."

Luther kissed her, then rose to his feet and fished for his handkerchief. "You've made me very happy, Lucy. I know it hasn't been easy for you. My Caleb can be like a penned bull when he feels he's being forced into something. But I've seen the way he looks at you. You two are a good match." His voice was full of satisfaction.

"I hope you're right," Lucy said quietly.

Percy came in dragging a chest behind him. He dropped it with a thump in front of Lucy. "Took me forever to find this, Boss. It was in the attic."

Luther reached over and opened the chest. Inside, shimmering silk dresses caught the sunlight.

Lucy gasped at the glorious array of color and texture. "These are far too grand to wear to cook in," she said, fingering a pale pink fabric.

"Nonsense, they've been tucked away far too long. You heard Percy. They were in the attic not doing a body any good." He pulled out the dress she had touched. "This will look lovely on you. You might as well surprise Caleb when he comes."

Lucy gasped at the reminder. She didn't have time to argue. "I must get busy. Thank you, Pa, I'll try to be careful of it." She gathered it in her arms and hurried to the spare bedroom. Water stood in the pitcher, so she quickly slipped out of her soiled dress, washed, and stepped into the clean dress. It was only as she began to button up the tiny seed pearls on the bodice that she realized it was the same dress Caleb's mother had worn in the picture in the box in his room.

She slid her hands over the smooth fabric. Would it bother him to see her in this dress? Maybe she should choose another. She bit her lip. There wasn't time to change. She would barely be ready for the men as it was. No, she would just have to wear this one.

Her boots were too muddy to put back on; she would just stick them on the porch to dry so she could knock off the hardened mud before she went home. In her stockings, she padded to the kitchen, depositing her boots on the porch along the way. Percy stood amid the pots and pans waiting for her.

Together they whipped together a beef stew with dumplings and apple pie using canned apples from the larder.

Percy tasted the stew. "You sure know how to cook, Miss Lucy. It does a body good to eat someone else's cooking for a change."

She smiled. At least this was one wifely duty she knew how to do. Before she could answer Percy, the door banged, and she heard the sound of men's voices. She could make out Caleb's voice amidst the babble, and her heart leapt.

"I'll set the table." Percy grabbed a handful of plates and dinnerware and rushed off to the dining room.

Lucy picked up the pot of stew and followed him. The

men's voices stilled when she entered the room. Her gaze picked out Caleb from the crowd of men. His laughter died when he saw her, and he frowned.

"Why are you wearing my mother's dress?" he demanded.

"My—my dress was soiled. I fell in the mud when the buggy got stuck."

"The bad man yelled at her," Eileen said. She slipped her hand in Caleb's.

His glower deepened, and he knelt beside the little girl. "What bad man, Sweetheart?"

Lucy bit her lip. She hadn't wanted Caleb to know.

"Lucy hit him with some mud. He was mad." Eileen spoke in a confiding tone of voice as Caleb lifted her into his arms.

"Lucy, what's this all about?" Still carrying Eileen, Caleb stepped next to Lucy. "Did someone threaten you?"

"Drew Larson stopped to help me get out of the mud," Lucy admitted. She would not tell him anymore than she had to. A range war had been started over less.

Caleb's expression darkened like a lowering storm cloud. "Did he touch you?"

Before Lucy could answer, Eileen piped up again. "Uh, huh. But Lucy got the gun."

"Lucy? What did he do?"

The entire roomful of men seemed to be holding their breaths. Lucy sighed. "He thought I ought to show a bit of appreciation for his help."

"I see. What kind of appreciation?" Caleb's voice was dangerous, and Lucy shivered.

"A—a kiss was what he had in mind."

Caleb ground his teeth together. "He's gone too far this

time. Stealing my cattle is one thing, but messing with my wife is another thing altogether. Monk, get the men together. We're riding to Burnett's ranch."

Lucy laid a hand on Caleb's arm. "Please, Caleb, I handled it. I warned him off with the gun. He knows I'm not easy prey."

"A man like that will be back." He shook off her hand. "Come on, men."

"Not Jed!" Lucy cried out in alarm when her brother moved as if to go with the rest of the men.

Caleb paused, then nodded. "You're right. It might be dangerous."

Dangerous! Lucy's heart clenched. She couldn't bear it if something happened to Caleb. It was all her fault. She should have told Eileen not to say anything, but she hadn't realized the little girl had seen so much. She had been sleeping when Drew rode up.

"What about dinner?" she called.

"Keep it warm."

Lucy sighed. She knew better than to berate him this time. But she could pray.

≥≈

Caleb's muscles were strung as tight as a tanning rawhide. His hands clenched the reins, and he urged his horse faster along the muddy road to the Burnett ranch. He prayed Burk Burnett was home. He didn't want to wallop the tar out of one of his men when he wasn't around.

Part of his anger was rage at himself. He should never have allowed Lucy to go out by herself; this was still very unsettled territory. Even Burk himself had only moved into this area last year. In addition to rough men like Drew

Larson, Indians still roamed, burning out the occasional settler. He needed to remember he was a family man now. His wife and her family depended on him to make proper decisions. This morning's had obviously been a bad one.

Several ranch hands milled around the corral as he stopped at the hitching post. He dismounted and tied his horse, then motioned for the men to stay where they were while he went to the door. He pounded on it with his fist. Only silence answered his knock. Pounding again, he took a deep breath. He had to stay calm and present his case to Burk in a reasonable fashion.

There was still no answer at the door, so he strode to the corral and watched two men working to saddle break a young mare. Peering through the dust and commotion, he finally spied Burk leaning against the fence by the barn as he watched the action in the corral. Clenching his fists, Caleb made his way to Burk's side.

Burk jerked his head up in surprise when he saw Caleb. In his early thirties, he had the keen eyes of a cattleman and a genial grin. Caleb had always liked him from the moment they met.

Caleb held out his hand. "Burk, I got some business with one of your hands."

Burk regarded him with a sober gaze. "Serious business, looks like."

"Drew Larson manhandled my wife today."

Burk's mouth pressed into a straight line, and his nostrils flared. "That so? Care to tell me about it?"

Caleb ignored the questions. "Where can I find him?"

Burk cocked an eyebrow. "I fired him yesterday. Caught him rustling cattle. That why you fired him?"

"Yep."

"I sure would have appreciated it if you would have let me know that. It would've saved me a heap of trouble."

"I reckon I should have, but I never like to meddle in another man's business." Caleb gritted his teeth. His quarry had flown the coop. "Got any idea where he is?"

"Town, most likely. He's probably trying to find some other sucker to hitch up with. I'm putting the word out not to hire him, though. We don't need his kind around here."

"I reckon I'll mosey into town and see if he's still around. I can't have my wife tormented."

"Congratulations on your marriage, by the way. I heard you got hitched, and she's a pretty little thing." Burk grinned and held out his hand.

Caleb shook it. "Thanks. I'm a lucky man." And as he walked back to his horse and mounted, he realized how true that was. How many other wives would have drawn a gun on a man like Drew Larson? And it wasn't just her fire and spirit that drew him or her exquisite beauty. It was something else, something that was all Lucy. Her fierce caring for her brother and sister, her determination to learn everything she needed to know to be a good rancher's wife, her moral backbone.

It had thrown him to see her in his mother's dress. He'd fingered that picture until it was about worn out. Until he'd seen her in Ma's dress, he hadn't realized how tiny his mother must have been, too. No wonder Pa wasn't afraid Lucy wouldn't make a good rancher's wife. He was always talking about how Ma had loved the ranch and how the men had adored and protected her. Lucy had that way about her, too. She drew people to her as naturally as bees to flowers. He glowered at the thought of how Drew Larson had dared to touch her. Digging his knees into his horse's side, he headed to town.

When he reached Wichita Falls, he stopped at the saloon and pushed inside. Larson was there, as he'd expected. He was talking to Curly Milton, a ranch owner from the other side of the county.

Larson flushed when he saw Caleb and the men behind him. His hand went to his holster, but he paused when Caleb pulled his gun first.

"No need for gunplay," he said, holding his splayed fingers out to show he held no weapon.

"Not this time, maybe," Caleb said. "But I'll not say the same if you dare come near my wife again." It was all he could do to not grab the man by the throat and throttle him.

Larson laughed, but it was forced and without humor. "I got no reason to seek out the pretty lady, Stanton. I merely stopped to help her out of the mud. If she says I did more than that, she's lying."

Rage tightened Caleb's throat. He seized Larson by the collar and hauled him to his feet. "My wife doesn't lie," he snarled. "I'm giving you just one warning, Larson. Stay away from Lucy. Better yet, you'd best seek employment somewhere else. You've just been blackballed in this county."

He turned to Curly. "This man stole cattle from me, Curly. I'd suggest you talk to Burk Burnett as well. He fired him yesterday for the same thing."

The man's bald head went pink, and his brows drew together. "In that case, I'll take my leave of you two." He stood and tossed some coins onto the table where they rolled against the plate and stopped.

"Hey, what about my job?" Larson called.

"I'm not interested in hiring a rustler." Curly clapped his hat on his head and strode out of the saloon.

Larson's lips drew back in a snarl like that of a rabid dog. "You'll pay for this, Stanton. You and that so-called wife of yours." He jerked out of Caleb's grip and ran from the building.

Caleb shouted and took off after him, but he had vanished. Frowning, Caleb ran for his horse. He would have to be more vigilant with Lucy. Larson was a dangerous man.

ten

The Wichita River, swollen from spring rains, rushed along beside their picnic spot in a tumble of water and flotsam. Lucy watched as Caleb tossed a ball with Jed and Eileen. Since he'd come back from confronting Drew Larson two weeks ago, things had been pleasant between them. Too pleasant. His gaze was admiring and gentle, but it was as though he was waiting on a sign from her. Several times she'd opened her mouth to talk to him about their relationship, then closed it just as quickly. She was a coward, and she couldn't bear for him to think her wanton.

They had family devotions each night, and Lucy was impressed at the amount of Scripture Caleb knew and at the depth of his wisdom. She'd wanted Jed to have a godly role model, and he adored Caleb. They attended worship every Sunday, making the drive to town like a normal family. But as she looked around at the other families who filled the pews, she knew they were like none of them. But she longed to be like the other wives, secure in a husband's love. She looked at Caleb playing with the children and smiled. God had been good to them so far. He would bring them the rest of the way to the fulfillment of all He planned for them. She could hold onto that certainty.

Caleb's hair fell across his forehead as he laughed and feinted away from Jed. Eileen squealed and threw herself against his leg. A smile tugged at Lucy's lips. She caught her breath at the wonder of her feelings. For the first time, she loved him as a wife should love a husband. Looking at his masculine arms, she desired them around her. He looked at her, and she felt the heat of a blush on her cheeks. Did he know?

Caleb reeled over with Eileen still clinging to him and collapsed on the quilt beside her. He closed his eyes. "I'm beat. We're supposed to be resting up before starting the roundup tomorrow, but I don't think this is the way to do it." He scooted over and put his head in Lucy's lap.

Lucy's cheeks heated, but she ran tentative fingers across his forehead, then lightly touched his thick hair. Caleb's eyes were still closed, and for that she was thankful. She stroked his hair, enjoying the feel of it between her fingers. She didn't want to think about the roundup tomorrow. Especially the branding. Her stomach congealed with dread at the thought. But Caleb needed all the help he could get.

"What time do we start tomorrow?" she asked.

"I told the boys to meet at the south pasture at six. Lord willing, we'll be done by suppertime on Wednesday. Since we're starting so early, Pa suggested we bring Eileen to him tonight."

"She'll keep him running."

"It was either that or he'd insist on helping with the roundup. At least this way, he feels useful, and Percy will help him. Eileen will be fine." Caleb sat up and sighed. "I reckon we should be going. Pa is expecting us for supper, and Bessie will be caterwauling to be milked."

Their idyllic day was at an end. She gathered up the remains of their dinner, then folded the quilt. Jed carried the things to the wagon.

That night she could hardly sleep for worrying about the coming three days. What if there were spiders when they slept out on the ground? And what if the ranch hands realized she was a tenderfoot and despised her for it? She wanted Caleb to be proud of her. Lucy sighed and rolled over. She could hear Caleb's soft snore above her head in the loft. He obviously wasn't worried about the roundup. And why should he be? He wasn't the one on display, the one everyone would be judging. An image of Margaret, tall and competent, floated before her like a gray cloud in the sky. Margaret would know how to handle herself on a roundup. All Lucy could do was disappoint.

Cheeper, the rooster, crowed at five, but Lucy was already awake. She hurriedly dressed in a pair of Jed's dungarees and one of his flannel shirts. They were both too big, but they would have to do. She couldn't do a man's work in a dress.

Caleb's brows lifted when he saw her attire, but he grunted in approval. "Glad to see you showing some sense about it," was all he said.

She fixed breakfast while he loaded the bedrolls into the wagon. The three of them ate breakfast in silence. Lucy kept stealing glances at Caleb's distracted face. He already had the cattle in his mind, she saw. After breakfast she followed him and Jed outside. The wagon was laden with the supplies for meals. At least part of her day would be spent with something she knew and loved. Bridget jumped into the wagon to join the fun.

The scene at the roundup was already chaotic. Cattle bellowed, and thick clouds of dust hung in the air. The air was fetid with the scent of cattle and manure. Lucy felt faint and nauseated, and the real work was yet to begin.

The men began to herd the longhorns together. Lucy mounted her mare and found her horse knew what to do better than she did. The mare cut and wheeled among the melee of horses and cattle while Bridget followed, nipping at the heels of the calves who tried to get away. They cut out the unbranded calves and herded them toward a corral the men had built.

Lucy took a deep breath as Rusty, the Stanton foreman, knelt to drop the branding irons in the fire. A movement to her right caught her eye, and she turned. Margaret Hannigan, her generous curves evident in her dungarees and shirt, laid her hand on Caleb's arm. His head was bent attentively to her.

Jealousy, hot and unexpected, swamped Lucy. What was Margaret doing here? She looked completely at home in those clothes. She laughed and tilted her head coquettishly to listen to something Caleb said, then walked toward the branding fire. Picking up a branding iron, she nodded for Rusty to ready the first calf.

The calf bucked and tried to run, but the two men holding bore it to the ground. Margaret walked to the calf and applied the Triple S brand. The calf bawled, and the sound smote Lucy's heart. She bit her lip so hard she could taste blood. The calf bawled again, and bile rose in her throat. Lucy turned to run, but her feet wouldn't obey her. A mist blocked her vision, and the ground rose up to meet her.

"Lucy!"

Hands shook her, but she kept her eyes shut. She didn't want to wake up; it was too early. She would just sleep a few more minutes, then get up to fix breakfast.

"Lucy, wake up."

Gradually she became aware of the hard chest she rested against and the feel of gentle hands holding her. The sounds around her penetrated her consciousness. Cattle lowing, men yelling above the din. Lucy opened her eyes and blinked. Caleb's anxious face swam into focus. Over his shoulder she could see Jed, and just past him, Margaret's concerned face.

Memory flooded back. That calf, the awful bawling, and the stench of burning hair. She felt faint again, and she closed her eyes. Tears stung her eyes and slipped from her closed lids.

Caleb's strong arm lifted her to a more upright position. "Would you like a drink of water?"

She nodded. Anything to avoid looking at the pity in Margaret's face. Pity for Caleb, for the burden he carried having such a sissified wife. He would be sorry he married her now. She sneaked a peek at his face through her lashes.

"Here, take a sip of water." He held a canteen to her lips, and she gulped it, then coughed as it went down the wrong way.

"Careful." He held it to her lips again, and she took another drink before she swiped the back of her hand across her mouth.

"Thanks." She finally dared to meet his gaze. "I'm sorry, Caleb," she whispered.

"Sorry for what? It's a bit overwhelming the first time. You're doing fine."

"The calf." Lucy gulped and broke off.

"I know. But the calf is fine. Look." He pointed to the little blaze-faced calf on the other side of the fence. It nuzzled its mother, then scampered off to play with a friend.

Relief flooded her, but the entire procedure still left a bad taste in her mouth. She let Caleb help her to her feet. Wooziness rushed over her again, and Caleb caught her as she would have fallen.

"Hey, Boss, 'spect you'll be having a little one scampering about, huh?" One of the men laughed, and heat flooded Lucy's face. If they only knew.

Caleb ignored the impolite comment and escorted Lucy to the wagon. She sank weakly onto the ground and leaned against a wagon wheel.

"You should have married Margaret," she muttered. She sensed Caleb go still.

"What's she got to do with this? Are you upset she's here? She always helps with our branding, and I help with theirs. She's just a friend, Lucy." His voice was stiff. "If you don't know I'm an honorable man by now, you don't know me at all."

She winced, and shame flooded her face. "It's not you; it's me," she said almost inaudibly. "I'm useless as a ranch wife. Margaret wasn't just watching, she participated. I will never be able to do that, Caleb." Her shoulders slumped, and she buried her face in her hands.

Caleb knelt beside her, and his breath whispered on her neck. His big hands took hers and pulled them from her face. "Lucy, I never asked you to do that. You're the one who's so determined to prove yourself. You don't have to prove anything to me."

She stared into his gray eyes doubtfully. "You said I was little and puny, that I couldn't be a good rancher's wife," she whispered.

"I was angry then, and wrong. Size doesn't matter, heart does. And you've got the biggest heart I've ever seen." His eyes were tender, and his hands cupped her face.

Her heart surged with hope. Did he mean it? His face came nearer, and her eyes fluttered shut. She held her breath and lifted her face. His breath touched her face. She waited in almost unbearable anticipation.

"Is she all right, Caleb?"

Lucy's eyes flew open at the sound of Margaret's voice. Caleb rocked back on his heels, then stood.

He held out his hand to Lucy. "She's fine, Margaret. Thanks for your concern. I'd best get back to the men."

His warm palm left Lucy's with obvious reluctance. Lucy forced herself to smile at Margaret. The other woman's gaze followed Caleb as he strode back to the dusty, noisy scene. She tore her gaze from Caleb's back with obvious reluctance and smiled distractedly at Lucy.

"I'd better get back, too." She dashed off without waiting for Lucy to reply.

Lucy turned her back on the commotion and began to sort through her supplies. She would not watch the woman ogle her husband. God would not be pleased at her jealousy. Caleb said he was happy with her the way she was. She would cling to that.

Dinner was nearly ready when she saw a buggy come rolling across the field. Shading her eyes, she waved at Luther and Eileen. Luther stopped the buggy at the chuck wagon and hoisted his bulk to the ground. Lucy went to get Eileen.

"Couldn't stay away, could you?" Lucy asked Luther with a teasing smile.

"In the ten years we've been ranching here, I've never

missed a roundup. I'm not going to start now." Luther's color was good, and his eyes were bright with excitement. "I think I'll go see if my boy is doing it right." He strode eagerly toward the men and animals.

"It smells," Eileen said. She wound her arms around Lucy's neck.

"I know, Sweetheart. But we'll stay here and get dinner ready." She put Eileen on the end of the wagon and stirred the stew one last time. She heard Eileen gasp and whirled to see what was the matter.

An Indian brave, dressed in buckskin and moccasins, stood by her sister. His brown hand was touching Eileen's shining golden locks. Eileen's blue eyes were wide, and tears trembled on the ends of her lashes.

Lucy sprang to her side and thrust her body between Eileen and the Indian. "Would you like something to eat?" she asked in a shrill voice.

The Indian's dark eyes narrowed, and he touched Lucy's blond hair with a curious hand. Lucy flinched away, and he frowned.

"How much?" He gestured at Eileen. "I give two fine horses for girl child."

"No! She is not for sale."

"I give you five horses." He reached for Eileen.

"No!" Lucy knocked his hand away. Trembling inside, she was determined not to show her fear. Where were the men? Didn't they see the danger?

The Indian scowled and stepped back. He crossed his arms over his chest. "Ten horses."

"No, not for a hundred horses." She scooped Eileen into her arms and dashed toward the safety of the men and cattle.

Was he following? Risking a glance back, she didn't see a rock in her path. Her foot struck it, and she went tumbling through the air. Lucy desperately tried to hang onto Eileen and to protect her with her own body.

Twisting as she fell, her arm hit the ground first, and she felt a sickening jerk inside. Crushing pain and nausea dimmed her sight to a pinpoint. She held Eileen against her with her good arm. A moan escaped her mouth.

Eileen began to sob and wail. Moments later Caleb knelt beside her.

"What happened? Are you all right?"

"My arm. The Indian," she babbled.

Caleb ran his hand over her arm, and she cried out when he touched her elbow. He bit his lip. "You've dislocated your elbow. I'll have to put it back in place." He stood and waved. "Margaret, could you help me?"

Lucy gritted her teeth. They wouldn't hear her cry out! She would show them what stuff she was made of.

Margaret held her hand while Caleb took hold of Lucy's arm, one hand on either side of her elbow. "Ready?" His face was white, and beads of perspiration stood out on his forehead.

"Yes," Lucy whispered. She closed her eyes and pressed her lips together.

Caleb jerked, and Lucy thought she would be sick. A scream hovered on her lips, but she refused to let it out. The pain was excruciating, and her vision wavered for several long moments. Then the pain began to ebb until it was a manageable dull throb.

Caleb helped her to sit. "You're a brave woman," he said. "What happened?"

Peering past his shoulder, she realized the Indian was gone. Her shoulders eased, and she sighed. Eileen was safe. She told Caleb about the Indian's offer for Eileen.

He sucked in his breath, and his face went white. "You're both beautiful and rather exotic looking to him. I'll have the men keep an eye out, and I want you to stay close to me."

He smiled, but his expression seemed forced to Lucy. She shuddered. He wouldn't have to tell her twice to stay close.

He stood. "You rest that shoulder. Margaret can see to finishing dinner."

"I'll do it." Lucy managed to get to her feet. Margaret wasn't taking over her job. She knew this competitive spirit she had toward the other woman was a sin, but she couldn't seem to help herself. Her elbow throbbed, but she pressed it against her side and hurried to finish dinner. She would prove to Caleb she was a better wife than Margaret if it was the last thing she did.

eleven

Caleb limped a bit as he walked toward the campsite. A blister had formed at his heel, his back felt like someone had stuck a pitchfork through it, and his left hand throbbed from a burn left by the branding iron. His bedroll was going to feel mighty good tonight.

The sight of the firelight on Lucy's golden hair made the glow of the campfire even more welcome. My, she was a beautiful sight. Her radiant hair fell to her waist, and he wondered what she would do if he walked up and plunged his hands into that glorious mass. Scream, probably. He was filthy, and he stank of cattle.

But he was blessed to call her his wife. His bemused grin faded. Unfortunately, that's all she was. A woman he called his wife. He'd watched for a sign from her that she was ready to move forward into a deeper relationship with him, but just when he thought there might be hope, she stepped back again.

She looked up as he approached. Her blue eyes were shadowed, but he didn't think it was from the pain of her dislocated elbow. She seemed to be using that arm a bit.

"I heated some water for you," she said. "Jed already washed up and went to bed."

"He worked as hard as a man today. You've done a good job with him." Caleb thrust his hands into the kettle of hot water, splashing it over his face and neck. "Whew, that feels mighty good."

"I brought a piece of pie from the chuck wagon. I thought you might be hungry."

"I'm almost too tired to be hungry. But pie sounds good." He took the pie from her outstretched hand and gulped it down in four bites. All he really wanted to do was crawl into his bedroll and rest his weary body.

The April air was muggy, even as late as it was. Staring into his wife's lovely face, Caleb felt all thought of sleep leave him. He pushed a log over to the fire and sat on it, then patted the spot next to him. "Let's jaw awhile. I'm not as tired as I thought I was."

She came toward him and perched on the log next to him. Her arm brushed his, and the contact sent a tingle up his back. "How's your arm?"

"Better. It still aches some, but the more I use it, the better it gets." She leaned forward and poked at the fire with a stick. Tiny sparks escaped the flames and shot upward into the dark night.

Caleb reached over and captured her hand. She jumped but didn't pull away. Instead, her slim fingers curled around his and returned his pressure. "I was proud of you today," he said softly.

Lucy jerked her head up, and her eyes went wide. "How could you be proud? I fainted at the sight of a simple branding, I ran shrieking in fear at the sight of an Indian, and then stumbled over my own feet and dislocated my elbow." Her voice was low and anguished. "I'm sure the men were laughing at the boss's poor choice in a wife. I came here to be a helpmeet, but it seems all I've managed to do is to be a hindrance."

"That's not true, Lucy. I'm glad you're here."

"Truly?" She turned to face him, and the movement brought her face only inches from his own. Her breath touched his face, and he caught a glimpse of perfect white teeth in the moonlight. Her breath was sweet and enticing. Something stirred in his heart; some new emotion had sprung to life.

He couldn't help himself. His fingers traveled up her arm to her mane of hair, and he pulled her into his arms. Caleb heard her soft gasp, and it only served to inflame the passion he felt for her. She fit into his arms as though she were made for him.

Her face turned up to his, and he pressed his lips against hers. At first Lucy was stiff, then she wound her arms around his neck and returned his kiss. His heart hammered against his ribs as he tasted the sweetness of her kiss for the first time. Caleb had never kissed a woman before, and the wonder of holding his wife in his arms this way drove all thought from his head.

He wanted to go on kissing her, but he felt her pull away a bit. "Did I hurt you?" he muttered in a hoarse whisper.

Keeping her face turned away, she shook her head. Was she crying? Caleb touched Lucy's chin with his fingers and turned her to face him. Her face was wet with tears, and his throat tightened. "What is it, Lucy?"

"Now you kiss me," she said softly. "Now when I've failed so miserably. I don't want your pity, Caleb. I want your love and your respect. You expected certain things from a wife, and I don't think I can ever meet those expectations."

"I don't have any expectations. I was wrong to lash out

at you that way. Wrong and pigheaded."

Lucy shook her head and knuckled away her tears. "You and Pa are building an empire here. An empire takes an empress, someone who can stand at your side and fight whatever comes without fear. Today has shown me I can never be that woman. I was wrong to think I could."

"This doesn't sound like the Lucy I know. Where's that spunky little woman who faced down the mongrel? Where's that gal who made me toe the line at mealtimes? I need you, Lucy. I just didn't realize it before." He twined a long curl around his finger.

"I wish that were true," she muttered. "You're so self-sufficient, Caleb, a self-made man. I have nothing I can bring you that you don't already have. I just didn't realize that until today."

He tried to pull her close again, but she stood and evaded his grasp. "Is this because Margaret is here? She's not the woman I want. You are."

"I don't want pity, Caleb. Margaret would have made a much better wife for you."

Caleb jumped to his feet. "I don't want Margaret," he shouted.

Several ranch hands glanced their way, and he lowered his voice. "The day I ever let you go, Lucy, is the day the Red River runs backwards." He turned and stalked away. Women! He didn't understand them. She was just getting tired of the isolation and hard work. Well, that was too bad. She was stuck with him.

He wandered through the maze of bedrolls and camp-fires until he reached the outskirts of the camp. Caleb wished Pa was here; maybe he knew more about how to

handle women. Lucy likely needed wooing, but he just didn't know how to do it, especially encumbered by her brother and sister. Not that he didn't love them, but sometimes a man needed space to say those things that only a wife should hear.

All he knew were cattle and horses, and they were easily handled by a cattle dog. He was out of his element here. If one of the newfangled universities offered a course on women, he would be the first to sign up. Lucy made his head spin with all her jawing and emotional turmoil. Next time she started talking like that, he'd just pull her into his arms and kiss her until she shut up. He grinned at the thought. She would likely toss a clump of mud at his head like she did Drew Larson.

He flopped down under a cottonwood tree. "I could use some help here, Lord," he said softly. "What do I do about this?" Caleb buried his face in his hands. In the stillness of the night, thoughts of Scripture crept into his mind, Scripture he thought he'd never need to apply to his own life.

Husbands, love your wives, even as Christ also loved the church, and gave himself for it.

The words wrapped around his heart. He'd admitted he cared for her, but did he love her? Caleb examined his heart. With dawning wonder, he realized he loved Lucy. She was the best thing that had ever happened to him. He didn't care if she never came on another roundup or ever learned to rope a calf. He loved her fire and determination, her desire to do right, just the essence of who she was.

What she did was unimportant.

But with a sinking heart, he realized he hadn't done a very good job of letting Lucy know that. All she'd heard was how important the ranch was to him, not how important she was, not how vital her happiness was to him. No wonder she was all wrapped up in performance and ability. He had to tell her how he felt and make it right.

But as quickly as the notion struck, he knew that was wrong. Words wouldn't convince Lucy. Actions were the only thing she would understand now. His actions had told her she was unimportant next to the ranch. Only actions would convince her she was the most important thing in his life. She would have to see the difference in him; then he would tell her he loved her. Not before.

❧

Lucy's heart ached in a most peculiar way. It was a good kind of hurt, the kind she felt when she probed a wound and brought out a splinter, the way she felt when her stomach burned with hunger but Jed and Eileen got up from the table with a full belly. At least she'd been honest with him. And he would come to agree. Maybe she could just be his housekeeper and give up any expectations of more. They could learn to get along that way somehow.

From here she could see Margaret's strong body, could hear her robust laughter. Margaret would have bred strong sons for Caleb. She could have stood at his side, shoulder to shoulder, and carved an empire out of this desolate place. Tears pricked Lucy's eyes, but she pushed them away. She was such a failure in all that she'd set her mind to do.

All her dreams of being a blessing to her husband were

gone. She had brought him nothing but aggravation. How had it come to this? Her high hopes and dreams of just last week lay in ashes from one day as a cowhand.

She kicked open her bedroll and sat down to take off her boots. Crawling under the blanket, she groaned at the hardness of the ground. She'd gotten spoiled in that soft bed Caleb had made for her.

As if the thought had brought him out of the fog, Caleb came through the smoke of the fire with an intent smile on his face. He said nothing, simply picked up his bedroll from the other side of Jed and laid it down beside her. He shifted it closer to her, then took off his boots and crawled under the blanket.

His arm snaked out from the covers and his fingers grasped hers. She waited for him to speak, to explain his intentions, but moments later she heard the even sound of his breathing. But even in his sleep, his hand still gripped hers. Lucy rolled over on her side and watched his face in the moonlight. She'd longed to watch him sleep for months. Now that she had the chance, there were dozens of people around. Lucy was so bewildered, she found it hard to fall asleep, in spite of her fatigue. But Caleb's presence beside her eased the fear she'd had of sleeping on the ground. No tarantula would dare bother her with his strong arms next to her.

Jed and Caleb were already gone by the time she awakened. Lucy sat up and rubbed the sleep from her eyes. The morning air was heavy with the promise of heat and humidity. A single spray of some kind of yellow wildflower lay on top of her bedroll.

"Caleb," she murmured. She picked up the flower. What

had gotten into him? He was acting almost romantic, which was totally out of character for him. She lifted the flower to her nose and breathed deeply of its fragrance. Sighing, she laid it aside and scrambled to her feet. There was a lot to do today.

She rolled up her bedroll and pulled on her boots, shaking them first to make sure no creepy crawlies had found their way inside. Taking her comb, she tugged it through her hair, then wadded her long tresses up on top of her head. Good thing she didn't have a mirror; the sight of her bedraggled state would surely be depressing.

When she made her way to the chuck wagon, most of the men were already out with the herd. She took a tin plate and scooped up a bit of the congealed gravy and hard biscuits. Lucy shook her head. If she'd awakened in time, she would have made some flapjacks. If the illustrious Margaret had made this breakfast, she wasn't as perfect as Caleb thought. She winced at her own unattractive thoughts. No wonder Caleb couldn't love her.

The mess had been left dirty, so she scraped the scraps onto a plate for Bridget and heated water to wash up. The bawling of the calves made her wince, and she thought about going back to the cabin. She was never going to be a proper rancher's wife anyway, so why prolong the agony? But Lucy couldn't force herself to go. Quitting was against her nature. Maybe today would be better. Caleb's gift of the flower had given her fresh hope somehow.

Lucy had just finished the dishes when Margaret came toward her. Striding like a man, her hair carelessly braided and tossed over one shoulder, she was the picture of health and vitality. Her white teeth flashed in her tanned face, and

Lucy had to smile back.

"I need a break," Margaret said. "My throat is as dry as gypsum. Any water handy?"

"Of course." Lucy grabbed a tin cup and scooped some water into it.

Margaret drank thirstily and wiped her mouth with the back of her hand. Lucy watched in fascination; she'd never met a woman who was so vital and alive. Margaret made no pretense of femininity, but she was attractive in spite of it.

Margaret plopped onto the ground at Lucy's feet. "You don't like me, do you, Lucy?"

Lucy blinked. "I—I don't really know you, Margaret. I'm sure you're a very nice person."

Margaret snorted. "Nice? That's the first time anyone ever accused me of that. Overbearing, manly, outspoken, those are terms I'm more familiar with."

Lucy opened her mouth, then closed it again. What could she say to that? It was all true, after all.

Margaret grinned at her obvious discomfiture. "Don't worry; you won't hurt my feelings none. Your problem with me is that you think I'm after your husband. You wouldn't be far wrong. But I know when I'm licked. He's in love with his pretty, genteel wife, and someone like me will never tempt him away."

In love with her? For a moment Lucy's heart soared, then thumped back to ground. Not likely. He felt something for her; she would allow that. But love? He loved his ranch, not her.

Margaret leaned forward. "I'm sorry to be so blunt, but we're going to be neighbors, and we need to clear the air between us. Yes, I was hurt when you came waltzing in the store on the arm of the man I had claimed as my own. Not that Caleb realized he was claimed, mind you, but I'd staked him out just the same. But I'm now sure it's for the best. Caleb and me are too hardheaded to rub along very well together. We would have always been clashing heads." She grinned. "Not that you haven't had your share of clashes from the sound of that argument last night."

Heat scorched Lucy's cheeks. "I—I do have a temper myself," she admitted. "You would make him a much better wife. Unfortunately, it's too late."

Margaret's eyes narrowed. "He loves you, Lucy. If you think there's anything between us, I'm telling you there's not."

"I believe you. I just can't be the helpmeet I should be. I wish I could be like you."

"So you're just going to give up like a yellow-bellied coward? Since when is marriage supposed to be perfect? Everyone goes into it with unreal expectations." Margaret shook her finger in Lucy's face. "Sounds to me like you're expecting more of yourself than Caleb expects from you. You need a dose of reality. Loving one another through arguments and sickness, through lean times and child rearing, that's reality. Perfection is like trying to catch a moonbeam."

Lucy stood. "You're not even married, Margaret. How can you presume to counsel me on marriage?"

"You're acting like a spoiled child who runs away when the other kids don't play her game. Grow up."

Lucy gasped. The woman had a nerve! Before she could think of a suitable retort, Margaret rose to her feet and swept her up in a bear hug.

"We'll be friends one of these days, Lucy. Give us both some time to lick our wounds. I like you; you got spunk. It's about time you showed it."

twelve

Lucy stirred the beans and then began to make cornbread for supper. The roundup was almost over, and she would be glad to get out of the dust and noise. And the smell! She wrinkled her nose. Margaret's words echoed in her mind. Did she expect too much of herself? Her parents had always expected her to be the best at everything she did. And she had to admit she took pride in doing more and giving more than other people.

Tears welled in her eyes, but she pressed her lips together and beat the cornbread batter as if it was the cause of all her turmoil. Tears never solved anything, but lately it seemed she was on the verge of them all the time.

While the cornbread was baking, she walked over to watch the last of the roundup. A thrill of joy shot through her as she watched Caleb astride his black gelding. He'd only bought the horse last week. A magnificent animal, man and horse were well matched. Caleb's powerful arms controlled the huge creature as an ordinary man would a pony, while his muscular thighs dared the horse to try to throw him.

Caleb's sandy hair was already beginning to lighten from the spring sunshine. He was a man who would turn heads no matter where he lived or what he did. No wonder Lucy couldn't measure up. She was a pale shadow of the kind of woman he should have.

Margaret rode next to him. She had that same vitality and vigor that Caleb possessed. But Margaret said she didn't want Caleb. How could any woman say that and mean it? Caleb had but to crook his finger, and any woman would want him. Lucy's heart clenched. She would never measure up; she would never be able to earn his love.

He wheeled on his horse and saw her. A tender smile accompanied the hand he lifted in greeting. Cantering over to her, he sat looking down at her from his saddle. "You've been in hiding all day. You getting used to the noise and commotion?"

She smiled. "I just thought I'd look to see how Jed was doing." And she had a need to see her husband, but she couldn't tell him that. She couldn't get enough of looking at him lately. What would he think of that, if he knew?

Caleb pointed out a group of riders across the field from them. "Rusty is teaching him to rope. He's picking it up pretty well, though on his first few attempts he managed to rope the fence post instead of the calf."

"You've done so much for him," Lucy said. "He actually likes work, and he's got a confidence I've never seen him show before. Thank you, Caleb."

The tenderness in Caleb's gaze sucked the breath from her lungs. The expressions on his face and the solicitousness of his manner for the past two days had Lucy pondering what was going on in his head. Was he really not disappointed in the bargain anymore? She was afraid to hope for that.

"Jed's a good boy. He'll be an asset on the cattle drive next week." He looked over her head. "Here comes Pa with Eileen."

Lucy turned and waved.

"I've missed her; she keeps things lively."

Lucy laughed. "I think things have been plenty lively around here."

"At least Pete didn't show up."

Lucy gasped. "Um, just where did you turn him loose?"

Caleb pointed to the far clump of trees. "Right there. Want to take a walk in the moonlight tonight and look for him? He might come if I call."

In spite of herself, Lucy felt the corners of her mouth turn up. "No thanks. I might have to ask you to stomp on him."

"I'd do it for you."

His gray eyes seemed to reach into her soul with an emotion she hadn't seen there before. What was going on in his head? A lump formed in Lucy's throat. "You—you would?"

His gaze caressed her face. "I reckon I'd do most anything for you, Lucy."

How did she answer that? A pulse beat high in her throat. Before she could make a fool of herself, Eileen and Luther reached them.

"This little girl is pert near pining herself to death for you," Luther said in a booming voice. "I tried reading her a story, and even Percy offered to let her help bake cookies, which was a big sacrifice since he never lets anyone in his kitchen." He caught Lucy's gaze. "Except for you, Lucy."

Eileen threw herself at Lucy's legs and began to clamber up them like she would a tree. "Lucy, we baked-ed cookies with raisins. Percy let me put the raisins in."

Lucy hugged her, relishing the feel of her small body. "You're getting to be a big girl, Eileen. Did you thank Percy?"

Eileen nodded her head, and her blond ponytail whipped in the breeze. She gazed up at Caleb's horse. "Can I pet him?"

"How about a ride on Morgan?" Caleb said. "Want to come, too, Lucy?"

Lucy glanced back at the chuck wagon. "I really should check on the cornbread." But the thought of being next to her husband for just a few minutes was almost too enticing to resist.

"I'll watch it," Luther said. "You go ahead with Caleb."

The pleased expression he wore brought a smile to Lucy's lips. Then the lightness in her heart faded. If he only knew the truth.

Caleb held out a hand. "Pa, you hold Eileen until I get Lucy up here, then she can put Eileen in front of her."

Eileen held out her arms to Luther. "Grandpa, you want to come, too?"

Luther lifted her into his arms. "No thanks, Pumpkin. That horse of Caleb's won't let just anyone ride him. You and your sister are special."

Eileen preened. "We're special, Lucy."

Caleb slid into the saddle, then gripped Lucy's hand and lifted her up in front of him on Morgan. Luther handed Eileen up to her, while Caleb reached around Lucy's waist and took the reins. He smelled of horse and leather with a hint of spice from his hair tonic. His breath ruffled her hair, and without thinking Lucy leaned back against his chest.

The shock of contact slicked her palms with perspiration, and she swallowed. She needed to stay away from close contact with Caleb. Touching him just made her realize all she was missing. Taking a deep breath, she started to ease forward, but his left arm came around her waist and pulled her closer. She could feel the hard muscles of his chest against her back, and he rested his chin on her head.

"Faster, Caleb!" Eileen kicked her little legs and giggled.

Caleb obliged by digging his heels into Morgan's ribs. The horse broke into a canter. Eileen loosened her grip on Lucy's arm and clapped her hands. They rode with the wind blowing the scent of sage and creosote in their faces.

Finally Eileen tugged on Lucy's arm. "I have to go potty, Lucy," she said in a loud whisper.

Lucy nodded and told Caleb. He pulled on the reins and stopped beside a rocky outcropping on the far side of the men. He slid to the ground and reached up to lift Eileen down.

"Wait for your sister," he told her.

His big hands spanned Lucy's waist as he lifted her from the saddle. Setting her on the ground mere inches from him, she had to fight an urge to wrap her arms around his waist and rest her head on his chest. What would he do if she did that? His gray eyes were somber, and his hands still held her. She swallowed and stepped away. Tearing her gaze from his, she turned to take Eileen's hand.

She was gone.

A rattle sounded to their right. Lucy turned and saw Eileen only two feet from a coiled rattler. "Eileen, no!" Lucy hurtled toward her sister. A split second later, the rattler struck at Eileen, but Lucy got there first. The snake's fangs sank into Lucy's right forearm, then pulled back for another strike. Eileen was shrieking, but Lucy felt nothing at first. Then a boom sounded, and a bullet slammed into the snake, driving its still writhing body away.

Caleb was there instantly, kneeling beside her. Two tiny puncture wounds oozing blood was all the damage Lucy could see, so she didn't understand why his face was so white. She felt fine; the snake must not have had much venom.

"Let me see." His voice was terse.

She cradled Eileen with her good arm and held the right one up like a child offering a gift. Dizziness suddenly swamped her. Then the pain struck, deep, burning pain. Lucy bit her lip in an effort not to cry out. She gritted her teeth against the pain.

Caleb took her arm in one hand, reaching into his pocket with the other. "Pa!" he bellowed across the field.

The rowdy, boisterous calls of the roundup faded until there was just Caleb's white face and Eileen's keening cry. Lucy held onto both to keep herself conscious. She mustn't frighten Eileen. Her sister clung to her, and she patted her hand weakly.

Caleb scooped Lucy up in his arms. Luther took Eileen, and they both ran with their burdens toward the fire. Caleb pulled his pocketknife out of his dungarees and heated it in the fire. He held it poised over Lucy's arm, an apology in his eyes.

His fingers bit into her flesh, but Lucy didn't cry out; the deeper pain of the poison was too great. She fought nausea and breathed deeply.

"This will hurt," he said softly. "I'm sorry, Love." Then the knife plunged down into Lucy's arm, and he made two slits over the puncture wounds.

The pain bit into her, and she cried out. Circles of blackness came and went in her vision. Caleb brought the cuts to his mouth. He sucked, then spat bright blood. Again he sucked the poison from her wounds and spat it out.

Time lost all meaning for Lucy as she watched her husband battle to save her life. She felt far away, as if this was all happening to someone else. Her vision blurred, and chills ravaged her. She tried to speak, to tell him not to do this. Caleb was risking his own life to save hers. If he had a cut in his mouth, the poison would kill him. She had brought him no blessing; she'd been a curse instead. But the words wouldn't come; her numb tongue was thick in her mouth. She closed her eyes and welcomed the blackness.

ès

"Yeehaw!" Caleb lashed the whip over the head of the horses as he drove the rig toward home. Her head on Jed's lap, Lucy lolled bonelessly in the back. Caleb didn't know another time he'd been this afraid. Not when the fire burned down the barn, not when the Wichita River flood came almost to the house. His knuckles white, he urged the horses to go faster.

Dust kicked up behind him as he jerked the team to a halt in front of the main house. Scooping up Lucy in his arms, he carried her into the house and up the steps to his old bedroom. His boot heels echoed emptily on the polished wood floors. Lucy's welfare landed squarely on his own shoulders.

He laid her in the bed. "Bring me that bowl and pitcher of water," he told Jed. Jed sprang to obey and brought the washcloth as well. Caleb loosened the buttons on her dress and began to sponge her with the damp cloth.

Lucy thrashed and cried out. Caleb felt helpless as he watched her agony. He wished he could take it for her.

Rattler venom could kill even a hardy man, let alone a tiny thing like Lucy. She was hardly bigger than a child.

The front door banged, and a minute later he heard his father's voice.

"Caleb, how is she?" His father's voice was loud in the quiet room.

"Still unconscious."

"Doc will be here shortly; I sent Rusty after him." His pa stood at the foot of the bed, his big hands gripping the bedpost.

"Where's Eileen?"

"Percy has her. He'll be along with her in a few hours, once we're sure Lucy is out of danger."

"*Will* she be out of danger, Pa? What if she doesn't make it?" The question was an anguished cry from his heart. He felt like a child again, needing assurance from the one stable thing in his life.

"She's in God's hands, Boy. It's up to the Lord. But we can pray right now and ask Him to spare her."

"What if He doesn't? How did you bear it when Ma died?"

Luther was silent for a moment, his gray eyes moist and faraway. "One day at a time, Caleb. I held onto God's hand and made it one day at a time." He leaned over and gripped Caleb's hand. "Let's pray, Son."

Caleb felt Jed's fingers creep into his hand, and he squeezed it with more reassurance than he felt. He bowed his head. "Oh, Lord, we can only ask for Your mercy right now. Don't take Lucy from us." His throat closed, and he couldn't speak. Jed gave a slight sob.

His thoughts were too jumbled to even voice out loud,

but he knew the Holy Spirit was there to speak them to the Lord. His father sniffled, and Caleb raised his head. They all stared at Lucy until the door banged again, and the doctor came bustling down the hall.

"How's my patient?" Doc asked, setting his black bag on the foot of the bed.

Lucy was so tiny; her feet came just past the halfway point of the bed. Her face was ashen against the white of the pillow. Doc examined her pupils, then pressed his stethoscope to her chest. Caleb held his breath and continued to pray.

Doc straightened up. "Her heart is pretty irregular, Caleb. I won't lie to you. It's going to be pretty touch and go through the night. Keep sponging her off with water and try to get some water down her as well." He gripped Caleb's hand and peered into his face. "How about you? Suffering any ill effects from sucking out that poison? Any sores in your mouth?"

Caleb shook the doctor's arm off impatiently. "I'm fine. Do you think she'll make it, Doc?"

The doctor shrugged, his brown eyes kind. "Do I look like God, Son? Sometimes I feel all I do is travel around to watch Him work. It's like offering a thimble of water to help the ocean. You are already appealing to the only One who can decide that." He snapped his bag closed. "There's nothing I can do for her, Caleb. She'll likely wake up soon, but she'll be hurting some. I'll leave some laudanum here to give her. If she gets worse, send Percy for me."

Caleb nodded, and Luther walked the doctor to the front door. Jed sighed and sat in the chair beside his sister.

Putting his face in his hands, he gave a huge sigh. Caleb put a hand on his shoulder. "We'll get through this together, Jed."

Jed raised wet eyes to meet his gaze. "What will happen to us if—if Lucy dies?" he whispered.

Caleb knelt beside him. "Jed, we're a family now, no matter what. But Lucy will be fine. We have to believe that. But I'll take care of you and Eileen. Don't you worry about that. I love you, Jed. You and Eileen both."

Jed flung his arms around Caleb's neck and burst into noisy sobs. Caleb pulled him tight against his chest and patted his back.

"What's all that caterwauling?" Lucy's voice was weak. She struggled to sit up, then whimpered. Gasping, she gripped her stomach, and her face went a shade whiter. "Water," she whispered.

"I'll get it!" Jed rushed from the room.

Caleb knelt beside the bed and touched Lucy's cheek. "Feeling pretty bad?"

"Like the barn fell on me." She tried to smile but moaned instead.

Caleb smoothed the hair back from her forehead. "You're going to be fine," he said. "The doctor was just here. We'll have some rough next few hours, but you hang on."

Her fingers crept across the top of the quilt and gripped his hand. "If I don't make it, Caleb—"

"Hush, don't even think that way." Now that she was awake, he felt a surge of hope, and not even Lucy could be allowed to dampen it.

"Jed and Eileen—"

"Don't worry about them. They'll be fine."

"But if something should happen, if I don't pull through this—"

Caleb caressed her cheek. "Rest, Love. I'll take care of Jed and Eileen."

Relief lit her face, then cramps struck her, and she doubled up in agony. Caleb felt helpless watching her suffer. Remembering the laudanum, he snatched it up and uncapped the bottle. He slid an arm under her and managed to get a swallow down her. Gasping, she fell back against the pillow.

Jed brought back the water, and Caleb gave Lucy a drink. Once she was sleeping again, he talked Jed into getting some rest, promising to call him if there was any change.

❧

For three days Caleb sat for long hours in the chair beside Lucy, offering her sips of water between bouts of sickness and sleeping. Her chills finally eased, and a bit of color began to come back to her cheeks. Caleb was bleary-eyed with fatigue, and when she closed her eyes, he dropped to the floor and rested his head against the mattress.

Lucy's fingers entwined in his hair. "There's room in the bed for you," she whispered.

He raised his head and stared down into her blue eyes. She'd made it over the hump; he could see it in her tender smile and pink cheeks. Without another word, she pulled back the quilt and scooted back against the wall. Caleb pulled off his boots and crawled into the bed.

He stretched out his arm, and Lucy curled up against his side. The sensation of someone else in the bed was a strange one, but something he thought he could get used to pretty quickly. Her breathing evened out, and he relaxed himself. She was asleep. Now if he could do the same. His mind whirled. When she was fully recovered, they would have to have a long talk. It was time to take up their lives together in earnest.

thirteen

An unfamiliar weight pressed against Lucy's waist, and she opened her eyes to find herself facing the wall in an unfamiliar room. She tried to move her arm and winced. The pain brought the memories flooding back. She looked down to see what pinned her in place and found an arm. A man's arm. Caleb's arm.

Shock rippled through her, and she eased away and sat up. Last night, his face had been tight with worry and fatigue. Now sleep had eased the lines and tension. A wave of love swept over her, and she reached over and smoothed the hair back from his face. His eyes flew open, and she stared deep into their depths.

A smile curved his firm lips. "Good morning. How do you feel?"

"A little sore and weak, but better I think."

He lifted his hand, and his fingers grazed her cheek. "You look lovely."

Heat flooded her cheeks, and she tore her gaze away. He couldn't mean that tender look he was giving her. She had to remember Margaret was his true love. It would be easy to mistake his concern for love.

'When do you leave for the cattle drive?"

"You eager to get rid of me?"

Her gaze flew to meet his again. "No, I want to go along."

146

His eyebrows arched, then he frowned. "The Chisolm Trail isn't for tenderfoots. I'll have my hands full looking out for Jed without worrying about you and Eileen."

"Someone will need to cook, why not me?"

"You just got bit by a rattlesnake. You hated the cattle and the dust of the past few days. The trail to Wichita will take three months." He crossed his arms. "You'll stay here and work on gardening and making curtains like a normal wife."

She laid a hand on his arm. "Please, Caleb. Am I that hateful to you that you can't stand to be with me?"

He groaned. "That's not fair, Lucy, and you know it. I've been trying to show you that I want this marriage to work. But the stress of the trail is not the way to do it." He swung his legs out of bed and stood. "It's out of the question. Now you rest while I fetch you some breakfast."

Lucy didn't answer, but a hard rock of determination grew within her. She'd failed at the roundup, but she would prove to him she could stand toe-to-toe with Margaret. Earning his love might not be easy, but it would be worth it. With God's help, she would conquer this weakness and go with him.

≥≥

By the end of the day she was longing for home. Home. Funny how she had begun to think of the cabin as her home so quickly. She hadn't had a home since her parents died, not a real home. Now she did. But it would never be the home she really needed until she could show herself worthy of Caleb's love.

Caleb brought the buggy to the front of the house, then escorted her out. His steadying arm around her waist would be easy to get used to. Jed helped Eileen clamber into the backseat while Caleb swung Lucy up onto the front seat. She felt naked without her bonnet, but it had been lost somehow in the excitement. The sun on her bare head was a welcome sensation. She still felt chilled and weak.

Was going on the cattle drive such a good idea in the condition she was in? She pushed away the doubts. This was her chance to prove herself; she had to go. She would enlist Jed's help and hide herself among the cowboys until it was too late to send her back. She shivered at the thought of Caleb's anger.

"Cold?"

She forced a smile. "Not really. The sun feels good."

"You won't say that come July and August. At least you won't be on the trail with the dust mixing with the perspiration until you look like you're covered in mud."

Doubt assailed her again. That didn't sound like much fun. But it surely wasn't as bad as he made out. He was just trying to make certain she didn't ask to go again.

They crested a hill, and the cabin came into sight. A curl of smoke rose in a welcoming spiral from the chimney. "Someone's started a fire," she said.

Caleb frowned. "Maybe one of the hands came over." He stopped the buggy in front of the house instead of the barn. Jumping out, he lifted Lucy down. His manner was brusque and businesslike as if he had something else on his mind. He helped her to the door.

The door swung open as they reached it, and Margaret's strong form filled the doorway. "Welcome home," she said with a smile. "Now, I'm not staying, mind you. But I thought after your ordeal you wouldn't feel up to cooking.

There's a roast and potatoes in the oven, and your bed is all ready for you." She stepped aside to allow them to enter.

"How thoughtful," Lucy stammered. And it was. So why did she feel so resentful? Margaret's overwhelming presence and many abilities just made Lucy feel even more inadequate.

"We sure do appreciate it, Margaret," Caleb said. There was affection in the nod he gave her.

Lucy saw the gesture, and tears pricked her eyes. How could Caleb ever grow to love her when she failed to attain Margaret's perfection? She was small and weak; she hated the noise and smells of the cattle; she needed rescuing every time she turned around. No wonder Caleb looked at Margaret with such admiration.

Weakness slowed her walk, and Caleb's grip around her waist tightened. He led her to the bed and made her sit down. Kneeling beside her, he slipped her boots off.

"Lie down. I'll get a quilt." He pulled a quilt from the rack and pulled it over her.

Margaret's face was filled with concern. "Can I do anything for you, Lucy?"

"No, you've done quite enough. Thank you so much, Margaret." Lucy lay back against the pillow with a sigh.

"If there's anything you need, just send Jed after me." Margaret picked up her basket and went to the door. "I'll check in on you tomorrow. Like I said, if there's anything I can do, send Jed to fetch me. Hopefully, you'll be almost yourself again by the time we leave for the cattle drive next week. Doc says your recovery has been nearly miraculous. And that's saying something for that old reprobate to let God take the credit for anything."

"You—you're going on the cattle drive?" Caleb hadn't mentioned that little detail.

"Of course. We're taking our cattle to Wichita, too. We always drive them together."

Hopeless. It was hopeless. How could she compete with Margaret's supreme competency? Lucy gritted her teeth. She *would* compete. She would compete and win!

Jed fixed her a cup of tea, and Eileen curled up beside her on the bed while Lucy read her a story from one of the books they'd brought in the trunk. If Lucy forgot the fact that Caleb wished he'd married Margaret, she could almost imagine they were the happy family they seemed. When they returned from the cattle drive, maybe they would be. She had to cling to that hope.

The scent of the roast and potatoes began to fill the air. Eileen had fallen asleep beside her, and Jed had gone outside to practice his rope throwing. He'd taken Bridget with him. The long-suffering dog would be his "calf."

She heard Caleb overhead in the loft. Scraping and banging, he seemed to be moving furniture. Curious, Lucy eased out of bed without awakening Eileen and went to the ladder leading to the loft. Though her head was still spinning, she clung to the ladder with clammy hands and managed to make her way to the loft. Peering over the top, she found Caleb with a broom in his hand.

He saw her and gave a sheepish grin. "I thought I ought to make sure there are no spiders up here before I leave."

"Why? You're not afraid of them."

"No, but you are. I'd like you to sleep here while I'm gone." His gray eyes were intent.

Lucy carefully finished the climb into the loft and stepped onto the rough floor. What did he mean? Her gaze probed his, and neither of them looked away.

"Then when I get back, I'd like us to share this room." His gaze never left hers as he took a step nearer.

Lucy's mouth went dry, and she was afraid to breathe.

"I reckon it's time we tried to make this marriage work." He was right in front of her now. He took a ringlet and twisted it around his finger.

But without love? Lucy wanted to ask him how he really felt about her, but the words stuck in her throat. Maybe he could grow to love her through the intimacy of marriage. He'd been different lately; maybe he was already beginning to love her. But no, she couldn't let herself hope. Hope always seemed to disappoint her.

"I love Jed and Eileen, but I want our own kids, too. I reckon that can't happen the ways things are right now." His thumb traced her jawline.

"I—I want children, too." She barely managed to get the words out past the lump in her throat.

"Girls with this pretty hair and your blue eyes."

"Strong sons," Lucy whispered. "With broad shoulders and gray eyes."

Those gray eyes crinkled in a smile, and his rough fingers caressed her cheek. "I won't mind if those girls are small and dainty like their mama," he said softly.

His face came closer, and Lucy closed her eyes and leaned against his chest. She was almost too weak to stand.

The front door banged, and Jed's voice rang out. "Hey, Lucy, Caleb, where is everybody?" His shout woke Eileen, and she began to cry.

Caleb sighed and stepped back. "I can't seem to woo my wife no matter how hard I try," he muttered. "Will you think about it, Lucy?"

Lucy opened her eyes. Unable to speak, she nodded, then went to the ladder and climbed down to see to Eileen. It would likely be all she thought about.

&

"Crown me." Caleb pushed his black checker toward Jed with an air of triumph. From the corner of his eye he could see Lucy moving about the cookstove. She seemed a little weak and shaky, but he thought she was mostly recovered from her snakebite. She'd insisted on fixing the meal. All evening the tension between them had grown. Should he ask her to share his room tonight, before he left for such a long trip?

He mentally shook his head. It was a fool notion. It wouldn't be fair to start a new life together, then leave her. Words of love seemed trapped behind his lips. In the loft he'd wanted to tell her she was his sun and moon, the one thing he would give all his possessions for. But such romantic words would have seemed strange pouring from the lips of a cowboy like him. He was no poet. But why couldn't he manage the simple words "I love you"?

Caleb had never thought of himself as a coward. But when it came to matters of the heart, he was at a loss. He dragged his concentration back onto the game before Jed could notice his preoccupation.

"Supper's ready," Lucy said. Eileen put her doll into the little bed Caleb had made for her.

Caleb stood. "Come with me, Eileen, I'll pump the water for us to wash up." He took the little girl's hand, and they went to the back door. As Caleb pumped the handle and water gushed over Eileen's then Jed's hands, he was struck with how dear this little family had all become to him. It wasn't just Lucy. God had surely blessed him; he'd just been too stupid to see it.

If he hadn't been so pigheaded at first, would things be different now? Maybe Lucy would not feel this fierce desire to prove she was as good as Margaret. He could see that was what drove her.

He sluiced water over his own hands and dried them on the towel that hung over the pump. As he went back inside with the children, he decided to just table all thought of his marriage until he got back. God would help him find his way through this morass of doubt.

After supper, they had their evening devotions together as usual, and then he climbed the ladder to bed. Tomorrow he would leave for Wichita, Kansas. Normally, he was full of excitement the night before a cattle drive. Now he hated to leave Lucy and Eileen behind. Maybe he should have allowed her to go, but she was so small and slight. He wanted to protect her; surely that was a normal response for a husband. He punched the pillow into shape and closed his eyes. He couldn't worry about it now; it was too late to change anything.

The next morning he was awake before Cheeper crowed. Noiselessly, he dressed and slipped down the ladder. He touched Jed's shoulder, but the lad was already awake. He sprang out of bed, a smile on his eager face.

Caleb looked at Lucy, still sleeping peacefully, one arm flung under her head. He knelt at the side of the bed and touched her forehead with his lips. Her eyes flew open, and he stared into the depths of her blue eyes. Every time he looked at the sky this summer, he would think of her. It would be hard to be away so long.

"I'm leaving now."

Pushing her heavy hair from her face, she sat up. "I'll fix you some breakfast."

"Don't bother. Jed and I will grab some biscuits. I'm not really hungry, and I don't think Jed could eat a mouthful. He's too excited." He leaned over and pressed his lips against hers, savoring their softness. Her arms went around his neck, and she clung to him.

"Pray for me. I'll be praying for you and Eileen."

A shadow darkened her eyes, and she nodded and averted her gaze.

He frowned. "Is something wrong?"

"No, no, of course not." She scrambled out of bed in a flurry of voluminous nightgown. "I'll walk you to the door."

At the door, he took her in his arms properly and buried his face in her sweet-smelling hair. "I reckon this will be the longest cattle drive in my life with a pretty wife waiting for me at home. I'll be back as quick as I can."

She nodded, and he gave her a lingering kiss before he stepped through the door. "Come on, Jed, we'll be late." With a final wave, he and Jed went to the barn and saddled their horses.

❧

As soon as Jed and Caleb were gone, Lucy flew into a flurry of activity. She dragged on a pair of Jed's dungarees. They were too big for her, but she cinched them in with a belt. The blue flannel shirt she had found in the bottom of the chest. It had been Jed's last year and fit her fairly well now. She stuffed her hair up in a kerchief to hide her hair, then covered it all with an old hat of Caleb's she had found in the barn. It was stiff and smelly, but it hid her identity fairly well. She stuffed extra clothing for her and Eileen in a bag, and then she woke Eileen.

"Where are we going, Lucy?" the little girl complained.

"A great adventure! We're going with Jed and Caleb."

Eileen thrust out her bottom lip. "I'm sleepy. We'll go tomorrow. And I don't like the cattle. They smell."

"If we don't go now, we won't see Jed and Caleb for a long, long time. Would you rather stay with Grandpa Luther?" Lucy had been toying with the idea of leaving her anyway. It would be a hard trip for a little girl. But Eileen had never been away from Lucy more than overnight.

Eileen considered, then nodded. "I love Grandpa."

Maybe she would be all right. Lucy had to make an instant decision. "All right. I'll run you over there."

She took Eileen's hand in one hand and snatched the bag with the other. She would have to hurry. Luckily, she could join the end of the herd and avoid Caleb for a few days that way. Saddling up Wanda, she hefted Eileen to the saddle, strapped on her bedroll and bag, then clambered up behind her. She'd never get used to riding this way. No matter how much she did it, she felt awkward and strange.

Cantering across the track, she headed for the main house. Minutes later, she pulled Wanda to a halt and slid down. Practically running, she hurried into the house. Luther was reading in the parlor.

His face brightened when he saw her, then his gaze took in her strange apparel. A smile tugged at his lips. "You're going with Caleb, aren't you? I knew you had spunk, Girl. You got any more clothes than that?"

"Only a couple of dresses."

"I got a trunk of Caleb's old clothes in the attic. Some of them will fit you." He rose and took Eileen from her. "I reckon I'm babysitting for young Eileen here. You and me will have fun, Chickadee." He tossed her in the air, and Eileen squealed.

"I really don't have time to look for more clothes," Lucy began.

"You got hours yet, Girl. The end of the herd won't pull out of here until close to ten by the time they all get rounded up and moving." He carried Eileen to the back stairway and opened the door. "It's that trunk at the top of the stairs. There's clothes there going back to when Caleb was a baby."

Rather than argue anymore, Lucy raced up the stairs. She threw back the lid of the trunk and rummaged through it. She would have to come back when there was time; the trunk was full of mementoes of Caleb's childhood. Rifling through small dungarees that would fit Eileen and tiny boots that she could imagine on her own child someday, she found three pair of dungarees she thought would fit her and four shirts. Hurrying back down the stairs, she went out to her horse and pulled down the bag. Pulling out Eileen's belongings, she stuffed the things she'd found for herself into it and carried Eileen's clothing inside.

"I have to go," Lucy told Luther. She knelt beside Eileen and hugged her. "You be good for Grandpa."

"Grandpa says I'se always good," Eileen said. She wrapped her arms around Lucy's neck. "Bye, Lucy. Don't cry. I'll take care of Grandpa."

"And I'll take care of our little girl. Now run along before all this blubbering is useless and Caleb is gone without you." Luther took Eileen from her and gave Lucy a slight shove.

After one final look, Lucy ran for her horse. Her heart pounded against her ribs, and she prayed to escape discovery. She had to make this work.

fourteen

The lowing of the longhorn cattle and the stench they left in their wake made Lucy begin to question her decision almost as soon as she arrived. The air was thick with red dust, and it was hard to breathe. Lucy coughed and pulled a red bandana up to cover her mouth.

"Hey, Cowboy, over here!" A weathered man Lucy didn't recognize waved to her, and she turned her mare's head to join him.

"You're late, Tenderfoot. You'll have to ride in the rear. You'll soon go runnin' home to mama." His face cracked in a grin, and the smile made him resemble someone, but Lucy couldn't decide who it was. "Round up them strays over there and watch to make sure they don't get away. My name's Bo, and you'll be answering to me this trip." Digging his knees into his horse's ribs, he wheeled and rode away.

Well, there was no time like the present to learn this cowboy business. Lucy set her chin and rode toward the stray cattle. They resisted her efforts to make them go the right way, and by the time she got them turned the right direction, she was wilting with dust and heat. The sun beat down in a merciless glare, and she longed for some shade and a drink of cold water. She'd remembered a canteen, but the water was warm and brackish.

Wiping her mouth, she pulled her bandana up again and got back to work. At times she felt as though she was barely clinging to the pommel as she grimly fought to do what was expected of a cowboy. Once she thought she saw Jed in the distance, but she pulled her hat down lower over her face and went the other direction. She couldn't risk even Jed's discovery.

When night fell, she was so stiff she almost fell from the saddle. Now she knew why cowboys walked bow-legged, she told herself with a grim smile. Hunkering down around the fire, she got her plate of beans and bread and retreated to the shadows again.

She wolfed down her food, then unrolled her bedroll and crawled under the blanket. She should wash up, but she couldn't find the energy. Lucy fell asleep to the sound of the men laughing and singing camp songs.

Morning came way too early. "Breakfast, Tenderfoot."

A hard boot in the ribs roused Lucy from sleep. She groaned and tried to sit up, but every muscle in her body cried out in pain.

Bo prodded her with his boot again. "Get up, or you can just head on back where you came from. We don't need no lazy boys on this trip. You're awful puny, Tenderfoot. I'm surprised your mama let you out to come with us. You're no bigger than a grasshopper. What's your name, Boy?"

Her name. She tried to pitch her voice low. "Uh, Luke, Sir."

"Sir. I like that. You are learning, Boy. Now get your lazy hide out of bed and get your breakfast. We pull out in half an hour." He walked away without waiting for an answer.

If she could just escape detection for one more day, she should be safe. Caleb wouldn't waste that much time to send her back. She forced herself to her feet and went to find breakfast.

The second day was a repeat of the first, with Lucy growing more confident on the back of the mare. She watched the others and learned to cut a steer out of the herd and how to drive strays back to the main group. Feeling rather smug, she stopped to take a swig of water and noticed a man driving two steers behind a rock. Thinking they would exit the other side of the rock, she watched, but they didn't emerge.

Alarmed, she rode over to see if something was wrong. A man was tethering the cattle together behind the rock. In a flash Lucy understood what was happening. A rustler! Anger gripped her, and she started to pull her rifle from its sling on her saddle, but then her hand stilled. What rustler would be afraid of a boy by himself, rifle or not? She wheeled her horse around.

But her movement had caught the rustler's attention. "Hey! Stop or I'll shoot!"

A bullet whizzed over her head, and she bent low over Wanda's neck. Another bullet whined by close to her cheek, and then she was out of range. Shaking with reaction, she saw Bo on the other side of the herd and made her way to him.

"A rustler!" she gasped.

Bo jerked his head up. His eyes narrowed as he stared at her. "Where?"

"Behind that rock." She pointed. "He has two cattle tied

up. He shot at me," she added.

His lips thin with rage, Bo rode off to where she pointed. Before he got there, a man on a horse tore out from behind the rock. He lashed his horse ferociously as he tried to get away. Bo shot over his head, and the man hunched down. Another cowboy rode to intercept the rustler, then another. Within minutes, he threw down his gun and surrendered.

Bo was berating him as he herded him back to camp. "I should have drowned you when you were born. How am I going to explain to Ma that you're a no-good cattle thief?"

The rustler turned his head and spat. "Shut up, Bo. I left home when I got tired of your lectures, and I'm in no mood for one now."

Drew Larson! That's who Bo reminded her of. They were brothers. Lucy hunched in her saddle. He might recognize her.

When his horse drew level to hers, he sneered at her. "A boy! Why couldn't you mind your own business, Kid? Stanton owes me; he would never miss a few head of cattle."

Lucy didn't speak; she was afraid her voice would give her away. Bo drove his brother on, pausing long enough to give her an approving nod. Lucy swelled with pride. She'd done well today. Wait until Caleb heard about it. Margaret herself couldn't have done better.

It was nearly dark when Bo rode back. Bo made his way to her side. "The boss wants to see you," he told her.

Lucy barely contained her gasp. "What for? It's bedtime."

"When the boss calls, there ain't no bedtime, Kid. You head on over there now." Bo's voice brooked no argument.

"I'll go in the morning."

Bo grabbed Lucy by the collar and raised her to her feet. "You'll go now. You got a lot to learn, Tenderfoot, and this is the main lesson. When the boss says jump, you ask how high." He released her, and she fell to the ground.

She rose, dusting herself off. "Yes, Sir." There was no help for it. She lifted her chin in the air. Caleb wouldn't send her back, not now. Her heart beat loudly in her ears as she saddled her horse and rode to the front of the herd. Maybe she had proved herself today; that's all she could hope for.

She found Caleb at the chuck wagon with Margaret beside him. Pulling her hat over her brow, Lucy dismounted and walked toward them. Staying in the shadows, she listened for a moment. They seemed to be reading the Bible.

"You mean, no matter how good I am, God won't let me into heaven?" Margaret's voice was indignant. "I've proven my worth to anyone who dared question it, Caleb Stanton!"

"God loves us for who we are, Margaret. We can't work our way to His love. That doesn't work here on this earth, either. You either love someone for who they are, or you can forget it. Love that is earned is no love at all. It won't last."

Caleb's word struck at Lucy's heart like an anvil. Was that what she'd been trying to do all her life? Even with God, she tried to be good, to be worthy of His love. Though she was certain of her faith, she realized she tried to prove herself worthy of His love and care. He loved her in her sin; why wouldn't He love her always?

And now with Caleb. . .she'd tried to work her way to his love as well. He either loved her or he didn't. And with

Caleb's words, she realized she desperately wanted to be loved just for being who she was, not for being like Margaret or like anyone. Just for being herself.

Her blood surged. She would find out now where she stood. If Caleb chose to love her, wonderful. If not, she would go on being the best wife she could, but with the gifts God had given *her,* not the ones He had given Margaret.

"You wanted to see me, Sir?" She kept her face turned down.

"You're Luke?"

"Yes, Sir."

"I reckon I owe you some thanks, young man. You've got sharp eyes."

"That's more than I can say for you, Caleb," Margaret observed. "That's no lad—that's a girl." She rose and knocked the hat off Lucy's head.

Lucy had wrapped a bandana round her hair to keep it from falling out while she worked and while she slept. But with the hat out of the way, she knew Caleb would recognize her anyway. Lifting her head, she whipped the bandana off and let her hair flow free.

Caleb gasped, and Margaret echoed it.

"Lucy!" Caleb rose to his feet. "What are you doing here? And where's Eileen?"

"I left Eileen with your father," she said. "I wanted to come with you, to prove I could do it, to prove I was as worthy a wife as Margaret."

"I think it's time for me to get another cup of coffee," Margaret murmured. She rose and left Lucy staring into Caleb's eyes.

"This was very foolish," Caleb said with a frown. "You're in no shape for this trip. I'll have to send you back."

"We've come too far. If you do, the drive will be delayed."

"I'll take you back myself," Caleb said. He rose and went to speak with Percy.

Lucy's spirits flagged. He wasn't even going to give her a chance; he was just sending her back without listening. Her shoulders drooped. She should have let Drew steal those stupid longhorns. At least she could have avoided detection until they were farther away.

Caleb came back. "We'll leave in the morning. You'd better get some rest."

There was a strange gleam to his eyes Lucy didn't understand, but right now she was too angry to care. She wheeled and stormed off. He could take her back, but he would have to listen to her on the way.

Before she'd gone ten steps, Caleb grabbed her arm and hauled her against his chest. "Where do you think you're going?"

"To bed!" she spat. "You don't want to hear what I have to say; you just want to pack me off home like a child."

Caleb gave an exasperated sigh. "Lucy, this just isn't the time or place. When we have this discussion, I don't want a camp full of observers."

Lucy glanced around, and heat crept up her neck. At least ten men were watching them with great interest. "Fine," she snapped. "We'll talk tomorrow."

"You're staying here. I'll send Jed for your bedroll and horse."

Lucy clenched her fists. "I've been doing just fine doing

my job. I'll continue with it until I go back."

"I reckon not. While I trust my own men, there are some here who signed on just for the drive. I'll not have you vulnerable."

"Fine. But keep away from me." She stalked over to a tree and flung herself down. If he thought he was holding her hand tonight, he could think again.

When Jed brought her bedroll, she kicked it open and clambered into it. But it was a long time before she slept.

By the time Caleb came for her the next morning, she was sitting on a tree stump sipping a cup of vile coffee. She'd coaxed some sugar from the cook, which was easier this morning than it had been yesterday, now that the cook knew she was the boss's wife. She longed for milk, though. Then the coffee might be drinkable.

When she saw Caleb, she poured out the rest of the bitter brew and rose.

"I'd pour it out, too, if it had sugar in it," he said with a teasing grin.

She shrugged. He needn't think he could smile at her and she would get over her pique with him. "I should have brought some tea."

His grin widened. "That would have given you away for sure."

Lucy's stiffness eased, and she chuckled. "That's what I thought."

He walked her to Wanda. "Those britches never looked that good on me," he whispered as he helped her mount.

Heat crept up her neck. What had gotten into him today? He seemed almost happy to be leaving the cattle drive.

They rode in silence to the south, back toward the ranch. At only twenty miles from home, they should reach the cabin by early afternoon. The cattle were only able to make ten miles a day, but the horses could do forty. Lucy wouldn't mind, she had to admit. That bedroll was hard.

Caleb finally broke the silence. He began showing her wildflowers along the way and told her their names. He pointed out the hawks flying overhead and the eagles atop the bluff they passed.

The landmarks began to be familiar to Lucy. They would be home soon. Would Caleb listen to her then?

Caleb cleared his throat. "Was Pa in on this all along?"

"No, he had no idea until I showed up that morning with Eileen. I had planned to take her with me, but she was sleepy and cranky, and I realized it wouldn't work."

"At least you showed *some* sense." He turned in the saddle and stared at her. "Why do you feel this need to prove yourself, Lucy? You have many talents; they just aren't with the cattle. I'm not saying you didn't do a good job as a cowboy. Bo said you were better than most of the tenderfoots he's worked with. But you hate it."

"But it's part of your life, and I want to share your life, Caleb. I don't want to be an appendage who has no relevance to your real life. Your real life is the cattle empire you're building. You said when we first met that you needed a wife who would work alongside you with the cattle."

Caleb sighed. "I was wrong, Lucy. I've told you I was wrong. I didn't know what I needed, but God did. I needed you."

Tears stung her eyes, but she sniffed and wiped her

nose on her sleeve.

They crested the hill, and Lucy saw the cabin in the distance. It looked abandoned and forlorn after only three days. The horses plodded to a stop in front of the barn, and Lucy slid to the ground.

"I'll go fix some dinner."

"I'll put the horses up." Caleb grabbed both halters and headed into the barn.

Despondent and heartsick, Lucy walked inside. Back again. She was a failure. After dinner she would have to go get Eileen. Her spirits lifted at the thought. She had missed her baby sister.

She opened a can of beef and added some potatoes and carrots from the cellar. It was hot by the time Caleb came in.

"Smells good," he said, shutting the door.

They ate in silence, then Caleb pushed back his chair and stood. He grabbed Lucy by the hand, and they walked to the sofa. That strange glint was back in his eyes as he sat on the sofa and pulled Lucy down onto his lap.

With his arms wrapped around her waist and his face buried in her hair, Lucy didn't know what to make of his strange behavior. Her heart was pounding so loud she found it hard to think, even hard to breathe.

Caleb pulled away and stared into her face. "What would it take for you to believe I love you, Lucy? Just like you are, warts and all."

"What warts?" Lucy smiled, but her smile faded at the gravity in his eyes. "What about Margaret?" she blurted out.

"What about Margaret? She's a childhood friend and a neighbor. Nothing more. You're my wife, Lucy. I love you."

Lucy gulped the tears in her throat. "You do? Truly? I overheard you talking to Margaret about love that is earned is no love at all. I realized that's what I've been doing my whole life. With everyone, not just with you. I've always felt I had to earn love. I think it started with my parents. Mama was always so strict and cold. I was the oldest, and I was supposed to do more, to give more. I always felt like a failure. But I want so badly to be loved for myself, for who I am."

Caleb's gray eyes grew solemn. "I love everything about you, Lucy. Everything that makes you who you are. Your fire and spirit, your determination to right any wrongs, your love for people, your compassion. I love you even if you hate tending cattle."

Lucy uttered a tiny cry and buried her face in his neck. He pressed his lips against her hair. "I'm so blessed God brought you to me," she whispered. "You're what gives meaning to everything I do."

His fingers lifted her chin, and he gazed into her eyes. "I love you, Lucy Stanton. I only hope our children are just like you."

His lips found hers, and she was lost in his kiss. It promised all the things she'd longed for all her life. A home, acceptance, and approval. She rubbed her hands across the rough stubble on his face, relishing his maleness and strength.

"I love you, Caleb. I've loved you for a long time, but I was so afraid you would never accept me. I'm never going to be like Margaret."

"I reckon I had plenty of opportunity to marry Margaret.

I always knew something was missing. You're more important than anything, Lucy, more important than the ranch even. What would you say if I told you I wasn't going back to the cattle drive?"

Lucy's eyes widened. "You have to go back!"

Caleb shook his head. "No, I don't. I have a good foreman and good cowboys. Percy will watch out for Jed. There's no reason to go back and a very good reason to stay." He cupped her face in his hands. "You are that reason, Lucy. It's been hard trying to woo you with Jed and Eileen in the house. We have that time now. Let's take it and get to know one another better. I love you, Lucy Stanton. I wish I was a poet, and I'd be able to tell you how much I love you."

With an inarticulate cry, Lucy burrowed into his arms. "I love you so much, Caleb," she sobbed. "I wanted to be a blessing to you, just like the Bible says."

"You already are," he murmured. "My life was empty without you. I can't imagine living without you. If you couldn't adapt to ranch life, I'd leave it all behind and find a job in the city. You're all I want, Lucy. You and Jed and Eileen. And our own kids, of course." He smiled crookedly.

"I love the ranch," Lucy said. "As long as I don't have to share it with Pete."

Caleb grinned. "Pete's gone, but you're here, and I'm here, Lucy. Can we have a honeymoon here or would you like to travel somewhere? I have money tucked away, if that's what you want."

"Keep your money, Caleb Stanton. All I want is you. This cabin with you is where I want to be. I won't have to share you with anyone here."

Caleb's eyes grew bright, and his lips came down to claim hers. Lucy reveled in his love and in who she was in his sight. She was the cattle baron's bride and proud of it.

A Letter To Our Readers

Dear Reader:

In order that we might better contribute to your reading enjoyment, we would appreciate your taking a few minutes to respond to the following questions. We welcome your comments and read each form and letter we receive. When completed, please return to the following:

Rebecca Germany, Fiction Editor
Heartsong Presents
PO Box 719
Uhrichsville, Ohio 44683

1. Did you enjoy reading *The Cattle Baron's Bride* by Colleen Coble?

    ❑ Very much! I would like to see more books by this author!

    ❑ Moderately. I would have enjoyed it more if

_____

_____

2. Are you a member of **Heartsong Presents**? Yes ❑ No ❑
   If no, where did you purchase this book?_____

_____

3. How would you rate, on a scale from 1 (poor) to 5 (superior), the cover design?_____

4. On a scale from 1 (poor) to 10 (superior), please rate the following elements.

    _____ Heroine   _____ Plot

    _____ Hero   _____ Inspirational theme

    _____ Setting   _____ Secondary characters

5. These characters were special because_____

_____

_____

6. How has this book inspired your life?_____

_____

_____

7. What settings would you like to see covered in future
   Heartsong Presents books?_____

_____

_____

8. What are some inspirational themes you would like to see
   treated in future books?_____

_____

_____

9. Would you be interested in reading other **Heartsong
   Presents** titles?   Yes ❑   No ❑

10. Please check your age range:
    ❑ Under 18   ❑ 18-24   ❑ 25-34
    ❑ 35-45   ❑ 46-55   ❑ Over 55

Name _____

Occupation _____

Address _____

City _____ State _____ Zip _____

Email _____

Ozarks

*F*our young women learn that there is no hiding from God—and love—in small towns among the rugged bluffs and clear-water lakes of Arkansas and Missouri. Amity and Emily face the biggest transitions of their lives, while Andrea and Carla fight the change that threatens their comfortable existence. Each of the four is about to embark on a journey of trust.

The road to contentment may be long and winding, like an Ozark highway. What does God have in store for each woman along the way?

paperback, 464 pages, 5 ³⁄₁₆" x 8"